A Winter Song

A Winter Song

DeNeece Butler

Printed in the United States of America on acid-free paper

ISBN-13: 978-0-578-80436-1 (hbk)
ISBN-13: 979-8-561871-23-8 (pbk)
ISBN-13: 978-1-393484-78-3 (ebk)

This novel is a work of fiction. Any resemblance to
actual persons, living or dead, or actual events is purely
coincidental.

When I began this journey with *A Winter Song,* as I wrote chapter after chapter, I would let my husband read them. As he is an ardent reader himself, I valued his opinion. He continued to deem it to be good and encouraged me to continue—and urged, and prodded, and nagged me to finish it. *A Winter Song* would not have become a reality without him and his encouragement. It is dedicated, therefore, as it should be, to the husband I love so much,

Cecil Victor (Vic) Butler

Acknowledgments

I first have to acknowledge my editor extraordinaire, Holly Monteith. Thank you, Holly, for your patience in working with a novice author and for all you have done to get this book finished and ready for market.

My dear friends Joanie and Gary Kilkelly stayed on my butt, almost as much as Vic did, to finish writing *A Winter Song*. Without their encouragement, it might not have happened. Our friend Mimi was so anxious to read the book, but the Good Lord needed her in heaven, and she did not get to read it. Maybe she can read it from there.

Wynne and Mary Adams are friends who, also, kept on me to finish. Mary did a little preliminary editing for me and pointed out things I had missed.

I am grateful to everyone who was interested and encouraged me to complete this challenge I gave to myself. I love you all. Thank you.

Part One

Chapter One

The screaming began with the sound of the braking tires of John Lassiter's car as he frantically tried to avoid an impending collision with the jackknifed semi truck sliding toward him on the steep, curvy mountain road. John's choices were to be hit by the semi, crash head-on into the rock wall of the mountainside on the right, or turn toward the deep ravine to the left. The screaming continued when Winter Lassiter was told that her parents, John and Grace, had been killed in a tragic auto accident. At one of the few places on the road where there was no guardrail, their car had plummeted down the mountain.

John and Grace were on their way to High Hope, the family home in the Appalachian Mountains of North Carolina, for the marriage of their daughter Winter to a young lawyer, David Earle Thorpe. David was fond of saying that there was an *e* at the end of his *Earl*. High Hope had been John's parents' home until his father, John Gordon Lassiter Sr., died in 1989.

His mother, Lila Lassiter, died ten years later. Lila had stayed on at High Hope alone after her husband's death, despite her son's pleas for her to move to Charlotte, North Carolina, to be closer to Grace and him. She insisted that she would die prematurely if she had to return to a city environment with all its pollution, heat, and hustle-bustle. She and John Gordon Sr., who went by his middle name, at least for Lila, had lived in Charlotte and raised John there. Besides, she had said, "Up on top of this mountain, at forty-three hundred foot elevation, I am closer to your father than I would be in Charlotte."

Everyone, it seemed, loved Lila. However, Lila and Winter had a very special relationship. Grace Lassiter had said that she didn't know with whom she had fallen more in love: her husband, John, or his mother, Lila. It was Lila who persuaded Grace and John to give their daughter the unusual name of "Winter." Her argument was that because it was an unusual name, she would be easily remembered. This turned out to be true enough. For all her life Winter fielded questions like "Winter? What kind of name is Winter?" And always, she would respond with an attitude that discouraged the questioner from pursuing the matter: "It is the name my grandmother gave me."

Furthermore, Lila said, Winter was her favorite season of the year, a time when one could rest, reflect, and dream. Her granddaughter should be named Winter, she said, because she was one of her favorite dreams come true. She had often dreamed about being a grandmother and showering a grandchild with that very special kind of love. Lila was always hard to deny when she got her heart set on something. So, Winter Lassiter it was. No middle name. Just Winter. Lila said girls didn't need a middle name. When they married, they could keep their maiden names as a middle name if they felt they needed one.

And shower Winter with grandmotherly love Lila did. As it turned out, Winter was to be the only child of John, Lila's only child, and the only grandchild she would ever have.

Names were important to Lila. She loved the alliteration of the *L*s in her own name, Lila Lassiter, and teasingly said the only reason she married Gordon Lassiter was because he gave her a beautiful name. He would get her back by introducing her as his first wife, implying there might be others to follow. The love in their eyes when they looked at each other belied any such notion. His name was John Gordon, and everyone called him John—everyone except Lila, who preferred Gordon as being, she said, "more melodic." It was not without an argument that she had allowed her husband to name their son after himself. For less confusion, if she insisted on calling him "Gordon," he insisted they would call their son "John." Just plain "John." She acquiesced to the special nature of a man having a son to carry on the family name.

She had named the farm "High Hope" because, first, it was high in the Appalachian Mountains. Second, it reflected her life's philosophy. "Where there is life, there is hope," she was fond of saying. Lila had pursued many parts of her life with little other than hope, but with so much determination, her "high hopes" were realized more often than not. The farm was a very important part of the lives of the Lassiter family, but particularly for the relationship between Winter and Lila. Winter begged to live there forever with her grandmother, but to no avail. All three of the loving adults in her life ganged up against her on that question. Her parents wanted her educated in a private school in Charlotte. Lila convinced her that restricting her visits to the mountains and High Hope only made them more precious. So, Winter resigned herself to being with her grandmother during summers, holidays, and frequent long weekends.

After Lila's death in 1999, High Hope continued to be maintained by Roy and Ellen Shands, a couple who had lived on the farm from a time soon after the Lassiters bought it and helped them with the work demanded by the house and land. Roy was a small, wiry man with physical strength his size belied. He had never been out of the state of North Carolina, and didn't care to be. Only a couple of times had he ventured down the mountain to Hickory, but he was ill at ease until he was, again, traveling the dirt roads of the rural mountain environment where he was born and raised. He didn't quite finish high school, but he was far from stupid. He had acquired a wealth of knowledge about the land, crops, farm equipment, and everything one needed to know to produce a profitable tobacco crop. He knew how to keep an old truck going beyond its manufacturer's intention.

One of the things that so endeared him to the Lassiters was his can-do attitude. If there was a minor plumbing or electrical problem at High Hope, he lit right into the task, whether he had any experience in that regard or not. He knew how to find out what he didn't know, but, more importantly, he knew the difference between what he did and did not know. When Lila referred to this quality in Roy, she liked to quote what she called a Chinese proverb: "He who thinks he knows, doesn't know. He who knows that he doesn't know, knows. For in this context, to know is not to know. And not to know is to know." She would quote; whoever was present would listen; then they would shake their heads with a "hmmm" and move on.

After several jobs in the construction trades, Roy settled into the job of High Hope's maintenance and farm manager and was as happy as "a hog in slop," as Lila put it. He loved the Lassiters, and they loved him.

Ellen Shands was as wide as she was tall. She and Roy could have been the original Jack Spratt couple. Ellen probably had a Slavic ethnicity in her background. She had a big-boned, strong body type, with wide shoulders and large breasts. All of her work clothes were worn thin in the chest, the result of her breasts getting in the way of her work. She looked like a woman who could have borne a litter of children with ease, but, unfortunately, she and Roy had only one son, Christopher. Ellen had developed a hematoma in her groin toward the end of the pregnancy and was bedridden for over a month. It was an extremely dangerous situation, and the doctor strongly advised against any future pregnancies.

Christopher was four years old when Roy and Ellen moved into a one-bedroom, one-bath cottage on the farm. It had originally been built for a spinster daughter of the former residents. When Lila and Gordon bought High Hope in 1978 to settle the spinster's parents' estate, she moved away from the area. Gossip had it that she had finally married a preacher in a small town nearby.

Lila, as is typical of a person of high intelligence and creativity, was scatterbrained and absent-minded. She informed everyone in the family that she was not scatterbrained but rather had a "chaotic cognition style." That's what a psychologist might have said. To everyone else, she was just plain harum-scarum in the manner in which she lived her life. It only got worse the older she got, and she depended more and more on Ellen, whom she called "her mind," to remember for her and to find things she was always losing. It pleased Ellen to be needed. Ellen's "cognition style" was detailed and organized. Together, she and Lila accomplished a great deal. And they loved each other in that special way women bond and understand each other. Ellen's job was to take care of the house at High Hope. It was a beautiful house that she truly loved keeping "spit-shined." She was only happy, she said, when the glass and metal were gleaming, the wood was glowing, and the textiles were bright.

Gordon Lassiter had been a successful architect. He and Lila met in college, where she was studying interior design. When they bought High Hope, it included four hundred acres of pristine mountain land; a small, sturdy log cabin built in 1912; the spinster's cottage; a barn; and some other outbuildings. Gordon had wanted to tear down the main cabin and build a new, modern home. Lila had wanted to remodel and add on to the cabin.

They had tried, early on in their marriage, to work together in their careers but found themselves unable to reconcile their tastes or philosophies. Lila would design a beautiful residence in a neo-Victorian style, her favorite, and Gordon would insist that, while it was beautiful, it couldn't be built economically with the available materials of the day and the rising cost of labor. Gordon grew to detest residential architecture and working with people whose desires and requirements for their residences made no practical sense to him. He preferred commercial projects, where economics and pragmatism reigned.

Lila, on the other hand, couldn't abide such heartless ventures and was in her glory designing a couple's home that would be an expression of the people they were and reflect their own tastes and lifestyles. Gordon and Lila's private debates were always lively and sometimes exasperating to both of them.

"Gordon, you keep forgetting the sacred three *Fs* of design: 'Form Follows Function.'"

"No, Lila, it is you who keeps forgetting the function of a home. It's a structure to keep one out of the rain and in which to keep one's things."

"That, my dear, is what a cave is for. Do you not think we have progressed further than our cave days? The function of homes can and should be so much more than caves. First of all, they are our safe havens, our islands in the midst of a stormy sea. The exterior walls of our homes are our protection, not only from the weather, but from the world at large. Our homes are like our last layer of clothing that affords us protection and privacy."

"Afford? Afford? What an interesting choice of words for you! You, who never seems to think about whether or not something is affordable."

"That's not the way I used the word, and you know it. Why must you always do that?"

"Do what?"

"Find some way to disrupt a point I am trying to make, especially when you begin to see that you have no valid argument for it?"

"That's not what I am doing, I merely—"

"May I finish?"

"Go ahead," he said with a deep sigh.

"In addition, one's home is a means of expressing one's values and tastes, another way of telling the world who one is. Why do you think there are so many different wallpaper patterns, paint colors, furniture styles, and such?"

"Is that a rhetorical question, or are you asking for a response?"

Lila, feeling herself ahead in this exchange, responded somewhat haughtily. "By all means, please do respond. I would be most interested in your opinion as to why we have so many choices of ways to decorate our homes."

"It's very simple. The more wallpaper books produced, the more room needed to use them, the larger a wallpaper store has to be, the more people have to be hired to sell wallpaper to the public, and so forth. It doesn't have as much to do with creative expression as it does with creating economic vitality and growth. It's about money, Lila."

"But, Gordon, don't you see that the impetus for the commercial activity, the first domino that fell, knocking all the others down, was the need for human expression?"

"Lila, I'll tell you what. I'll continue designing the shopping centers, and you continue taking clients to the wallpaper stores in them. You do your thing, and I'll do mine." That debate turned out to be pretty much a standoff between them, as most did.

And so it would go with Lila and Gordon. They were both right, of course, and both of them knew it. They frequently argued their different points of view, however, mostly for the purpose of the interaction between them, the mental stimulation, the emotional connection. It was with the decisions surrounding the approach to their joint residence at High Hope that required one point of view or the other to prevail. Lila won. The main cabin was remodeled and enlarged.

There were two entrances to the farm. For the main entrance at the beginning of the long driveway up to the house, Lila had stone walls built with professionally made signs of the name of the farm installed in the middle of the walls. At the end of the walls were stone pillars with stone flower pots set on top. Flowers were planted in the strips in front of the walls.

For the back entrance, there was a plain metal gate that opened to a dirt "pig trail" alongside a babbling creek. When Lila and Gordon first purchased the property, this back entrance led to a shack, with a very old truck parked in the weeds. The seller of the property told Lila that a woman used to live there, and when he went to tell her the property was to be sold and she needed to make arrangements to move, he found her sitting on the front porch eating something from a can that had obviously been opened with a manual can opener. A couple of children dashed off into the woods as scared animals might have done. Also, in the creek was an old rusted truck, an appliance, and several other things that had been discarded. The shack needed to be torn down and all the rest needed to be hauled off. Her local building contractor said he knew of a "feller," Frank, whom he thought would take care of this for her, and told her where he lived, which was nearby.

She went to where the contractor had told her to go. She found another dwelling just this side of being another shack. The yard was full of discarded items: auto parts, cans, trash in general. There was a toddler, naked except for a diaper hanging low, full of urine, playing among the trash with an oil can in his hand. Ignoring this, Lila knocked at the door, which was answered by a man with a week-old beard and a dark shirt with an undershirt that had been white at some point in time but had become soiled to dark gray. Someone else might have made a hasty retreat from those premises, but Lila had been known not to be afraid of the devil himself. She introduced herself and explained why she was there. He wanted to see exactly what she was asking of him, so he got in his truck and followed her to the farm.

Lila had learned how to communicate with these backwoods mountain folk. Going slowly was the best way. She showed him what she wanted to have removed. He agreed, and a generous price was established. Then Lila said, "I've 'bout figured out how that truck got into the creek. It must've slid off the road when it was icy."

"No," he said, scuffing his foot in the dirt.

"No? Then how did it get down there?" She, too, scuffed her foot in the dirt, waiting for a reply, which was slow in coming.

"Just to get it out da way," he said.

Frank came to the house to announce that the job was finished and wanted Lila to see if it satisfied her. So they both went in her car to the back gate property, which had been cleared of everything she wanted gone. When they returned to the house and Frank's truck, the contractor was on the roof of the addition, giving him a clear view into Lila's car. Frank had placed his hand on Lila's knee and was patting it, telling her that if she needed anything else done, just to let him know. From that point forward, the contractor teased Lila about having a boyfriend!

The residence at High Hope turned out to be a rustic mountain house, built with half logs, Victorian gables, and wrap-around porches that came together at one corner in a gazebo with a turret-style roof. Fish-scale shingles of various shapes adorned the front and back gables. To simulate classic Victorian gingerbread for the porch and railings, native Rhododendron limbs were used, with their curves and twists. "A Barney Flintstone porch," Gordon called it. Lila persuaded Gordon to leave the fireplace in what was the front room of the original cabin, remodeled into a large eat-in kitchen. Lila had always wanted a fireplace in her kitchen. A second fireplace was included in the new living room. "A waste," said Gordon. Lila said that a home needed lots of fireplaces because it provided the comfort of one of the four elements: fire, water, air, and earth. Perched up in the air on a mountaintop, with several streams below, Lila had her fireplaces and all four elements around her.

The Shandses were hired and moved into the spinster's cottage during the middle of this major remodeling, soon after Lila and Gordon had purchased

High Hope—not the best way to begin new jobs and a relationship with new employers. By the time the house was finished and moved into, the Shands and the Lassiter family not only survived the stress of it all, but had become close. The Shandses became part of the Lassiter family over the years, part of all Winter's memories of High Hope.

Lila's death in 1999 crushed the entire family, Winter particularly, who was at the tender age of fifteen. It was a comfort that the Shandses were there, as they had always been, when the Lassiters and Winter continued to come to High Hope at every opportunity.

John and Grace had been very pleased with Winter's choice for a husband, David, but not overly thrilled with her choice of places for the happy event. Formerly, Winter and David had decided to wait until their careers were established before they thought of marriage to anyone. Besides, while they both dated and had busy social calendars, neither had met anyone they considered to be a life partner candidate, until they had met each other.

There was no question in Winter's mind about where the ceremony would take place. Of course, this very special time of her life would take place at the most special place of her life, High Hope, as close as she could come to the most special person in her life, her grandmother Lila Lassiter. The fact that most of the wedding guests lived in Charlotte was lost on Winter. She had inherited her grandmother's stubbornness when it came to matters of the heart. Logic be hanged! She finally did concede to setting the date for her marriage in a season other than winter. Winters in the mountains were always unpredictable and varied from year to year. It could be fifty-five degrees on a sunny January day or blizzard conditions in April. Winter and David decided on June 17 for their wedding day. That would be time enough, she reasoned, to make the flower beds and rose bushes beautiful, as she and her grandmother had done every year, and as Winter continued to come to High Hope to help the Shandses do every spring after Lila's death. They would be married in the gazebo, at the last moments of sunset.

As she was pondering this decision, she suddenly remembered a time shortly after Lila's death when Roy Shands had asked John Lassiter about the disposition of Lila's body.

"John," Roy said, "I've been meanin' to ask 'bout somethin'. Miz Lila's memorial service was real nice. I don't want you'uns to think it wuddun'. But . . . it's just that nobody's real sure about where her body is. We know she died in California and that she had donated her body to science, but after they were done with it, why wuddun she buried here at High Hope? Or she coulda been cremated so's we could spread her ashes around here on the farm. Ya' know how she loved it here. I know the doctor who tended her was s'posed to be real good. But . . . sometimes, I cain't help but wonder if her heart didn't quit just 'cause she was gone from up here. Anyway, I hope you don't mind my askin', John, but . . . where is her body?"

Winter recalled that her father had quickly turned his face away from Roy and paused a long time before responding. When he did respond, she was startled to see her father's face drained of blood and to hear him stammer, "Roy, we all have to know that she is still here in spirit." There was another pause, as though he were about to say something else, but instead, he suddenly turned and walked away. Roy looked after him without a satisfactory answer to his question. He didn't press the issue, assuming from John's reaction that it was still too painful for him to discuss. Winter wondered about this even many years later. There was much about her grandmother's death, though, that seemed sort of . . . mysterious.

It was June 11, less than a week before the wedding. John and Grace were on their way to High Hope to join in the flurry of activity in preparation for the wedding. Ellen Shands, watering flowers in the gazebo, first saw Sheriff Red Potter's patrol car pulling up the driveway.

Red Potter's father had been the sheriff, and Red

was in his own fourth term as sheriff. Both father and son had been good sheriffs, taking their jobs very seriously. Red had inherited his father's shock of red hair, which, of course, produced the same nickname for both of them. Their given names were the same as well: Nathan Earl. Red Sr. was called "Red," and Red Jr. came to be known as R.J., except when he was called "Red" like his father. Some said that the only reason Red Jr. was elected sheriff was because folks were so accustomed to knowing their sheriff as Red Potter. They even looked very much alike, with their graying red hair, fair complexion with a few freckles remaining into adulthood, and a little on the lanky side, with a small pot belly trying its best to develop into something substantial. When Red Sr. retired, it was natural for Red Jr. to carry on as sheriff. Everyone in the county knew R.J., and he knew each family as well, including the Lassiters.

Looking back on it, Ellen never could figure out why she immediately called for Winter when she saw R.J.'s car, rather than going to greet him as she normally would have. Something—a sudden, terrible sinking feeling in the pit of her stomach—grabbed her. She somehow knew he was the bearer of bad news. In some inexplicable way, she just knew. The expression on his face as he slowly climbed the steps to the porch confirmed that feeling.

Winter, thinking her parents had arrived, hurried to the porch.

"Mom? Dad?" she called. Instead of her parents, she found R.J. and Ellen standing and staring at each other silently.

"Oh, R.J.," Winter said lightly but tentatively. "I thought Mom and Dad had finally arrived. They're late. How are you? It's good to see you."

"Winter—" R.J. dropped his head and fell quiet, as though he couldn't bear to hear the words coming out of his mouth. Now Winter knew. Somehow she knew but couldn't accept it. In total denial of the pain that had begun to swell within her, she continued lightly.

"R.J., I'm so glad you stopped by—or did Mom call you? Ellen, did you call him? We had on our to-do list to talk to you about traffic next week for the wedding. You and Alma did get the invitation, didn't you? A couple of people didn't, and I had to resend—"

"Winter!" R.J. had gathered his nerves and resolve. He had to tell her. "Winter," he began, "honey, I'm so sorry. I have some bad news to tell you."

Ellen's body slumped. She grabbed the porch rail for support. Winter began shaking and, after a moment, in a harsh whisper, asked, "What, R.J.? What is it?"

"It's your mom and dad, Winter."

"Are they all right? Where are they?"

"No, honey. They're not all right. There was an accident on 321. With a semi that lost control and started sliding sideways down the road."

Ellen reached for Winter and held her tight, the two of them clinging to each other for support, both needing to be held upright.

"Are they hurt? Where are they?"

"Winter, honey—" Again R.J. paused, wanting more than he wanted to breathe not to have to say the words. "Winter, they were both killed in the accident."

Winter stood and stared at first, disbelieving what she had heard. Ellen gasped and immediately began to sob. R.J. moved toward Winter, who rebuffed his offer of comfort, as if to accept it would confirm the truth of what he had told her. She took a step backward, uttered a simple, quiet "no." Then she turned her back to them, grasping the porch rail. From somewhere deep within her came a scream of one word that could not only be heard but could almost be seen as the pain of it leaped out across the lawn, beyond the driveway, up and over the surrounding mountains.

She screamed, "*Grand-mo-ther . . . !*"

Then again.

And over and over again, until she collapsed in an hysterical heap into Ellen's and R.J.'s arms.

Chapter Two

The heat in Charlotte that June 14 was unbearable. As Winter sat under the tent at the burial service for her parents, the tears and droplets of perspiration streaming down her face were indistinguishable. She felt dizzy; the minister's voice seemed far, far away. The only things that seemed real to her were the unspeakable pain that gripped her mind and her fiancé's hands, clasped together with hers.

What attracted her to David at the very first were personal qualities without which she felt she could never have survived the tragedy that caused them to postpone their wedding. He was there for and with her as he had been from the moment they met, when, as a young lawyer, on behalf of one of his clients, he needed to avail himself of the services of the young psychologist Winter had become, in preparation for a closing argument in court that was to take place later that day. He explained that he had a situation with an eyewitness who testified emphatically about what he saw but was, in fact, mistaken. He wanted Winter to advise him about the psychology of such a person and how he could counter that testimony.

After David explained the details of the situation, Winter thought for a moment, then realized this was a matter of perception being mistaken for reality. She picked up the crystal egg she kept on her desk and handed it to him. Winter told him that it was a gift from her grandmother, who'd told her that as she turned it in the light, its colors changed. This, her grandmother told her, was to remind her of the difference between reality and perception. The crystal egg could appear to be different colors, but that was only perception. David asked if he could borrow it, as he thought it could be useful to him in his closing argument that was to take place at two o'clock that afternoon; he asked her if she would like to come to the courthouse to hear it and make sure her crystal egg was returned to her. After a check of her calendar for that afternoon, and finding that it was clear, she agreed, and also agreed to his invitation to join him for lunch before going to the courthouse. The attraction between them was immediate and powerful.

David's client for whom he was offering his closing argument had been charged with armed robbery and first-degree murder. The facts of the case appeared to be very much against his client. There was a witness, a murder weapon, a bag of money on the ground, and a motive. The crime had taken place at a convenience store in a poor part of town where unemployment was extremely high, and where his client lived.

The victim was the owner of the convenience store. It was the third time he had been robbed, only this time, he had obtained a gun, which he'd kept beside the register, hidden underneath some paper bags. The facts the prosecutor presented were that at approximately one thirty in the morning, David's client, James Graham, had entered the store wearing a ski mask, jumped behind the counter with a knife, and demanded the money from the register. The owner, Dan Whorley, gave him the money, but then as the robber was approaching the door to leave, Dan drew his gun and fired, missing the robber and hitting the glass door, which shattered. The robber was startled, swirled around to avoid the shattering glass, and fell. He quickly got back to his feet and dashed out the door with Dan on his heels, gun in hand. The robber turned the corner at the end of the building, and Dan, still in chase, turned the corner as well, only to be suddenly knocked to the ground and stabbed in the abdomen by the robber, who had been waiting for him there. The prosecutor claimed that James Graham was that robber. He further claimed that a witness drove his car up to the store with headlights showing a light-skinned black man in a black hoodie raising the knife to stab Mr. Whorley. The witness instantly shifted his car into reverse and, looking behind him, drove to what he thought was a safe enough distance to dial 911. In a lineup, the witness picked out James as the man he had seen stabbing Mr. Whorley, even though James was wearing a dark blue hoodie rather than a black one, as the witness had previously said.

The defense, offered by David Thorpe, told a different story to the jury. James was employed as a construction cleanup man. He was working toward his college degree in architecture and studied late at night. He was married, had a ten-month-old baby girl, and lived nearby. He frequented the convenience store and knew Dan Whorley well. On the night in question, he was about to go to bed when he noticed the empty diaper box his wife had left on the kitchen counter to remind him to go to the store for diapers. The prosecutor made a big deal out of this explanation. Who buys diapers at one thirty in the morning? A young man who had forgotten about getting the diapers until after having studied for several hours, that's who, asserted David Thorpe.

What the witness had seen for just a few seconds before he quickly turned his head to back up and go to where he felt safe was James pulling the knife out of Dan's abdomen rather than stabbing him with it. James had arrived at the corner just as the robber was rounding it to run away after having stabbed Mr. Whorley. They bumped into each other, knocking James off his feet and causing the robber to drop the bag of money. Scared, the robber just started running rather than stopping to pick it up. When James got back to his feet, he saw Mr. Whorley lying on the ground with a knife sticking out of his abdomen.

When the police arrived, they found James bending over Dan, putting pressure on the stab wound with his hands after having removed the knife, which, of course, should not have been done. He was afraid to remove his hands from Dan to get his cell phone out of his pocket but then was grateful to hear sirens heading his way. His first words to the officers who arrived on the scene was to plead for them to call an ambulance for Dan. When they insisted that he get on the ground to be handcuffed, he angrily told them they needed to keep pressure on the wound until the ambulance arrived. The officers whom David called to testify at the trial confirmed what they had heard James say but construed it to mean only that he had become afraid that he had actually killed Dan. That was the only explanation they could come up with to explain why James didn't just stab and run away.

David began his closing statement with humor.

"A woman," he said, "caught her husband in bed with another woman. In his defense, the husband asked his wife, 'Are you going to believe me, or your lying eyes?'" After the giggling from everyone in the courtroom subsided, he continued. "So what is the truth?" David asked the jury. "What is the reality and what is perception? Can a person have 'lying eyes,' believing what he has witnessed to be accurate and true, or has what he seen been misinterpreted?

"You have heard testimony from James' employer, the professor who was teaching him online and confirmed that James had submitted his test at about one fifteen that morning. You have heard testimony from several character witnesses, telling you that James couldn't—wouldn't—do such a thing. So, what are you to believe?"

With this David took the crystal egg he had borrowed from Winter, held it up in front of the jury, and slowly turned it around. "Is this crystal egg blue; is it pink; is it lavender? That depends on the angle at which it is being observed. One of you might declare that it is blue. Another of you from another angle might be quite sure it is pink. And so it is in this case. What did the witness actually see? Reality or merely perception? Is the truth, as the prosecutor has asserted, that James Graham, having a wife and child to support with minimal earnings, decided to rob Mr. Whorley, who unfortunately died as a result of the stabbing and, therefore, can't tell us who thrust the knife into his abdomen? Were James Graham's fingerprints on the knife put there by stabbing Mr. Whorley, or by pulling it out of him?" As David spoke those words, he picked up the knife in question from the evidence table, raised it, thrust it, then raised it again, as though to pull the knife out of Mr. Whorley's abdomen. "Was the hoodie the perpetrator was wearing black as the witness testified, or was it dark blue as testified by the officer who booked James into jail?

"Ladies and gentlemen, I submit to you that this is a case of mistaken identity, mistaken interpretation of what was witnessed, mistaken assumptions by the officers responding to the scene and by the prosecutor. I submit to you that James Graham is completely innocent of having robbed and killed his friend, Mr. Whorley, and that what has been suggested to be the truth is actually mistaken perception."

As David delivered the last sentence of his closing argument, he once again lifted the crystal egg and turned it slowly round and round.

"The defense rests," David said. The jury took only two hours to find James Graham innocent of all charges against him. James and his wife cried. David smiled broadly. Winter sat in total adoration of this man who had almost instantly stolen her heart.

Winter "talked" to her grandmother frequently, knowing full well that she remained close to her. Once when Lila was still alive, there had been an accident when a close family friend had fallen off the roof he was repairing and died from a broken neck. Soft-hearted Winter was terribly upset about this. She asked her grandmother why God let such things happen, why people were killed in hurricanes and tornados and accidents.

"Winter, sweetheart, come sit here and let's talk about that. What I need you to understand is that there really is no such thing as death."

"No such thing as death, Grandmother? What do you mean? People and animals die all the time."

"No, honey, it is just that their bodies have worn out or hurt beyond repair. But, we are not our bodies. We are spirits who only use these bodies to experience our five senses, sight, sound, touch, smell, and taste, and to express our feelings. Our spirits are made of energy. Later on in school you will learn about matter and energy, and you will learn that energy cannot be destroyed. Our bodies are matter and our spirits are energy. Our bodies can be destroyed, but not our spirits. For now, think of it this way. We could go get some ice and put it in a pot on the stove. Think of the ice as matter, our bodies. Then we turn on the burner and the ice melts and becomes water. Something has happened to change the matter, as if it died. But, then, as the water boils away, steam rises into the atmosphere. Think of the steam as our spirits. Through this process, matter was changed, leaving energy, and that energy, our spirit, can never be destroyed."

Winter listened attentively and mostly grasped what her grandmother was explaining to her. It occurred to Lila that while her own death was not impending, she was aging, and if life proceeded in what was deemed to be a normal way, she would die while Winter was still alive, and Winter would be shattered by that. She continued talking to Winter.

"And Winter, the wonderful thing is that when our spirits are separated from our bodies, we continue to exist in our spirits. We can go where we want to and see the people whom we have loved, and sometimes the energy of that love can even intervene in a real way in the lives of our loved ones. You know, Winter, that one day I am going to die. But here's what you need to remember. In my spirit form I will still be close to you, watching you, loving you, and protecting you."

"Oh, Grandmother, that time is a long, long way off, right?"

"Right. Now let's go see what Ellen is doing and if we can help."

And off they went to find Ellen.

Sometimes, in especially quiet moments, Winter thought she could hear her grandmother's voice in her own head commenting on what Winter was telling her. She told her about David. As she had explained to her grandmother, it gave new meaning to the phrase "love at first sight." This was one of those times when Winter thought for sure she could hear Lila respond, "Is there really any other kind?"

David and Winter had decided only three short months after they had met to marry, but that was only for the sake of their families. Left on their own, they would have become as legally married as they had become emotionally married after their first two weeks together. They spent the next few months planning for a wedding in June. They allowed their parents to meet each of them before they announced their engagement. Then, there was the "getting the families together" part, which resulted in the happiness of all in David's and Winter's choices for a life mate.

David Thorpe came from a fine family—everyone said so—a long line of lawyers and judges. Winter had cared little about that. She came from a "fine family," too. Nor did she care all that much about the fact that he was truly handsome and well built, with dark hair, dark eyes, and a wonderful smile that quickly and frequently exploded on his face. She was good-looking, too. She had inherited her grandmother's thick, curly

auburn hair, fair complexion, and brown eyes, which
could have a golden cast to them or be almost black,
depending on what she wore, what light she was in,
or how she was feeling.

Since Winter's father, John, was a lawyer, he was
especially thrilled about David being a criminal defense
lawyer, although criminal law had not been John's cup
of tea. David's parents, Richard and Elizabeth Thorpe,
lived in Atlanta. Rich, as his friends called him, was
a judge, and Elizabeth's vocation, according to David,
was "Atlantan Southern Belle Socialite." Winter found
both to be charming, and she was not nearly as put
off by his mother as David had thought she would be.
Perhaps this was because Elizabeth was in a "state of
approval" about her son's choice of a daughter-in-law
for her. The biographical information about Winter
David had given his mother was immediately acceptable as a person who would fit into Atlantan society.
Upon meeting Winter, Elizabeth was pleased to see
that she was beautiful as well, which meant, of course,
that Winter and her handsome son would give her
beautiful grandchildren.

Winter and David realized full well that a marriage
was not just between two individuals; rather, there
needed to be a blending of the two families for a
marriage to be most successful. They realized this, but
whether their families blended with each other was

not going to determine whether they married. There was only one person's opinion Winter truly cared about: her grandmother's. She knew that when she took David to High Hope, she could sense her grandmother's feelings about him. Winter had explained to David that he couldn't truly know who she was until he had gone with her to the mountains, to High Hope, to her grandmother. They had seen each other every night of their first two weeks together. They had made rapturous love. Their hearts had become united. By the third weekend, Winter knew it was time to go to High Hope. Her parents had not even met him yet. First things first.

Chapter Three

It was a Saturday morning in late March when David drove his red Porsche higher and higher up the mountain roads. Winter always experienced feelings of calm and excitement, both at the same time, as she got closer and closer to High Hope, a feeling difficult to explain, something akin to relief. While David had been to the mountains before, it was as though this were the first time for both of them. They looked at everything with a sense of newness. They looked at everything through eyes of love.

When they finally turned into the long driveway toward High Hope, Winter playfully began tooting the horn. Ellen greeted them with open arms. Winter had told Ellen and Roy about the very special visitor she was bringing. Ellen, true to her nature, rose to the occasion with the preparation of a wonderful lunch, a "fancy" lunch in the dining room with all Lila's finery. Roy had been instructed to be on his best behavior for Winter's "young man from the city"—no overalls or farm boots at the table. Roy had stopped his fence repair work to become clean shaven and Sunday-dressed in new overalls for Winter and David's arrival. With a twinkle in his eye, he had inquired of Ellen if a fancy lunch was all he was going to get for the trouble. Ellen, with a twinkle in her eye, popped him good with a wet dishcloth.

Conversation at lunch was the typically pleasant, "getting acquainted" kind of talk. Dawdling over coffee, David said, "Winter has told me so very much about High Hope, you folks, and her grandmother. Miz Lila sounds like someone I regret very much not having had the opportunity to know."

"Not another'n like 'er," Roy was quick to reply.

"Oh, that's true enough," joined Ellen. "She was a remarkable person. Not a day goes by we don't think about her and miss her. She's been gone now . . . what is it, Roy?"

"Seventeen year. She died seventeen year ago. We've missed 'er ever' day of that seventeen year." Roy dropped his head lest another man should see the lack of manliness in the sadness of his eyes.

Ellen reached over to pat Roy's hand and continued telling David about Lila. "Nothing much has been changed in the house. Oh, we paint, and freshen up as need be. But, basically, ever'thing is just as Lila left it. Even her clothes are still in her closet. Once in a while

I wash up all her clothes that's washable, and send the rest to the cleaners. John thought it an awful waste, so I stopped tellin' him 'bout it and just paid for the cleaning on my own."

Ellen glanced at Winter with a knowing look. Of course, Winter had known about this and paid for the cleaning herself most of the time after she had her own income. It had been their secret. Ellen continued.

"I know John was right. It is a waste of money. But it makes me feel so much better when ever'thing in her closet's clean and ready for her to put on. Makes me feel, oh, I don't know, like she'll walk in any minute and ask me where is this or that in her closet. God bless her, she never could find a thing!"

Winter could feel a swell of emotion rising within her with this talk of missing her grandmother, so she tried to change the subject.

"How is Christopher? Let's see, he's going to be thirty-six next October, isn't he? That's right, isn't it, because he's four years older than I, and I'll be thirty-two this year."

Before Ellen could answer, Winter turned to David and continued. "Christopher and I almost shared a birthday. He was born October 3, and my birthday—don't you dare forget it—is October 5. All the years we were growing up together, we celebrated our birthdays together on the fourth."

"How did Christopher like having to wait a day to celebrate his birthday?" asked David.

"Typical lawyer question!" Winter laughed.

Roy was the next to speak. "There did come a time—oh, I think it was when Christopher was 'bout ten—that he noticed he always celebrated his birthday a day late and didn't like it much. Miz Lila took care o' that, though. From then 'til he went away to college, they'd always go off and do somethin' special on the actual day of his birthday. That seemed to satisfy him, and he never made a fuss again. She was always doin' for him."

Ellen joined in. "Doin' for him ain't the half of it. David, you want to know about Lila Lassiter? I'll tell you something."

Winter resignedly poured herself another cup of coffee. She could see there was no getting away from Lila stories. But, then, this is what she wanted David to learn. So large a part of who Winter was as a person was a reflection of who Lila had been.

"She stayed on us and Christopher about the importance of education. Education. Education. 'That boy has to have a good education to get along in the world that's comin'. No matter where he winds up. Here or some'rs else.' She was always telling us that. Well, we were all mighty pleased and proud when he graduated from high school, but we didn't have the way to send him to college, what with it costin' so much 'n' all. So what does she do? I'm not exactly sure how she pulled it off, but she talked to some people and got him a scholarship for half his tuition and books, and she paid the rest. Set up some kinda trust fund for his education. So, he went to college and graduated. By the skin of his teeth, but he did graduate. That's the sort of person Lila Lassiter was. Did you know 'bout that, Winter?"

"Yes. I knew. She didn't tell me, but I heard Mom and Dad talking one time and sort of figured it out. I don't think she told anyone other than Mom and Dad."

Roy shook his head in confirmation of Ellen's story. She was nearly worn out from the telling of it and stopped for breath. David asked, "Where is Christopher now? What is he doing?"

Roy replied, "He's gone up to Tennessee buildin'. Turned out to be a buildin' contractor. Says he likes it real well and seems to be good at it. Truth be known, I always thought that was Miz Lila's doin's, too. I used to hear her tell him what a fine occupation it was to build homes for folks."

"I'll look forward to meeting him someday soon," David said.

"Well, Mr. Thorpe," Winter interjected, "in the meantime, you come with me. There are so many places on the farm I want to show you."

Roy began helping Ellen clear the table as David and Winter started off on their jaunt.

"I'd still like to know where Miz Lila's body was laid," Roy muttered.

"She's in California, Roy. John told us that," Ellen responded.

"Well, no, he didn't 'xactly say that. Anyway, if she was buried in California where she had gone on vacation with her friend Susan, why cain't she be dug up and brought home where she belongs? I never will understand."

"I know, hon. I'm not sure I do either. Somehow I think her friend Susan—you know, the one she went to California with? She visited here once in a while? I think she had something to do with Lila not being brought home."

Roy grunted and said something about it just not being right.

Meanwhile, Winter was giving David the grand tour of all her favorite places on the farm: the ridge with its spectacular view, the orchard, the cattle, the creek, the acres of Frazier fir Christmas trees, and other places that were special to her and her grandmother. Especially the fifty-bush rose garden. Winter started giggling when they got to that site. When David asked what she was giggling about, she explained. As Lila got older, she refused to let anyone take her photograph. She said it was like looking at a five-day-old rose in a vase with its petals falling to the table top. Very sad.

Lila was always getting dressed to go see someone, and just before getting into the car, she'd decide to go cut some roses to take with her. There she was one day, in the rose garden in her best clothes and jewelry, with her tattered old garden hat on her head, cutting roses. Sometimes clouds would hang low over the mountains, and on that day, they were spilling over in the cut between two mountains peaks. It looked like a washing machine had been overfilled with detergent and suds were spilling out over the tub. Winter said she happened to be on the deck of the house with her camera to capture this scene when Lila saw her there and raised a rose to show her how beautiful it was. Winter quickly snapped the photo, which was used for the portrait that hung over the mantel in the living room. Lila didn't care for it but did say that the artist had done a good job.

The end of the tour brought them to one of the car-sized boulders by the creek, listening to its gurgling flow.

"So?" Winter asked.

"So what?"

"So what do you think of my High Hope and Ellen and Roy?"

"High Hope is more beautiful than you had described. I can see why you love it so. Ellen and Roy are . . . delightful."

"You hesitated. What is it about Ellen and Roy that made you hesitate?"

"Oh, I don't know. I've only just met them, but . . . —I begin to understand what a special person your grandmother was, but . . ."

"But what? Come on, out with it."

"Well, that business about Ellen keeping up your grandmother's clothes. For seventeen years! I'm sorry, that just struck me as, well, sort of odd, in the extreme."

Winter smiled and looked off into the distance for a moment before she responded.

"I know. I know how that could seem odd. You say you begin to understand about Grandmother, but there was just so much to her. I'd give anything if you could have really known her. Anything at all. I was fifteen when she died, and I have so many wonderful memories of her. Mom and Dad do, too. We all love to tell Lila stories, as you'll find out when you meet Mom and Dad. I guess Ellen and I keep her clothes because in that silly way we fleetingly fool ourselves into thinking she's just gone to visit her friend Susan and will be back soon. It's just too painful to imagine that she's really gone for good. It may not make sense, but then, why does it have to?"

David looked long and hard at this woman with whom he had fallen so deeply in love. As the sun shone through the trees, her auburn hair glistened. When she spoke of her grandmother, her face took on a faraway expression, a poignant wistfulness that tugged at his heart. After a long moment, he took her in his arms, gently rocked her, and whispered, "It doesn't, baby. It doesn't have to make sense. It only has to make you feel good. Like you make me feel good, just by being you." They kissed and then made love on that huge boulder, in the dappled sunlight, with a cool October breeze blowing across their half-clad bodies, never knowing that in eight months, instead of experiencing the joy of their wedding day, they would be sitting under a tent in a cemetery in Charlotte, trying to say good-bye to her parents.

Not everyone could fit under the tent. There was a huge crowd at the funeral and at the cemetery. All the wedding guests were there, crying tears of sorrow instead of feeling the joy they had been anticipating. Most of them were standing in the June sun and so were grateful that the minister's graveside service was brief. Each person filed by Winter. Most could not speak for crying; they could only touch her, hoping she could feel the love and sorrow in their touch.

At last, it was time to go to her parents' home to receive the mourners who had been invited for refreshments. Then and there, the first moments of healing began. Sweet stories about John and Grace were told. Some laughter could be heard here and there. A huge crowd from their church, where Grace had been so active, was there. Of course, so also were Ellen, Roy, Christopher, and his wife, pregnant with their first child. Everyone from John's law firm was in attendance. Tom Dougherty, John's law partner of twenty years, was there. He quietly told Winter that he would be available any time convenient to her to help settle her parents' estate. John and Grace had been greatly loved. Their lives had been well lived.

In due course, Tom Dougherty had guided Winter through the business of her parents' estate. It was fairly straightforward. The sizable estates of Lila and Gordon went to their only child, John. John and Grace, then, had been quite astute in managing their financial lives, with the estate comprising several real estate holdings to be disposed of in time and a healthy stock and bond portfolio. It had all been left to Winter, except for a large trust fund for Lila's friend Susan. Winter didn't question that bequest. Even with that reduction of the estate, including what John and Grace had inherited from Gordon and Lila, Winter had suddenly become a very wealthy young woman, with an extremely comfortable income from the estate's assets.

Ellen and Roy helped her dispose of whatever contents of John and Grace's house she didn't want to keep, and the house was put on the market for sale. David and Winter's wedding at High Hope was, of course, postponed, then canceled. Instead, she and David were quietly married at the courthouse by a judge who had been a friend of her father. Winter had already moved into David's apartment, where she stayed until they could decide where they wanted to live.

At their last meeting, Tom Dougherty told Winter there was one other matter he had not handled directly for her parents. He told her she would need to see her grandmother's attorney, Henry Campbell, about it.

"What is it about, Tom?" she asked.

"Winter, I'm not quite sure. All I can tell you is that John had me put a memo in his file to remind me to tell you that you must see Henry Campbell after the deaths of both him and Grace. As I recall our conversation about it, it has something to do with your grandmother's remains. I see Henry over there, but you'll probably want to talk with him some time other than this. I'm sure Henry can enlighten you."

"Well, okay. We're going to High Hope next week. I'll call him then."

"Good! Good! You let me know, now, if I can help you at all. Just let me know."

"I will, Tom, and thank you. David and I will be having a party in the next few weeks, sort of a belated wedding reception for ourselves. We'll hope to see you then."

"We'll be there with bells on. Don't you worry about that!"

They hugged, and Winter left.

And that was that. Almost all the things that need to be done as a result of someone's untimely death had been accomplished. Now, at last, she and David could go to High Hope. She had already decided for herself how and where she wanted them to spend the rest of their lives. In Bliss, the small mountain town she loved. To live at High Hope. All she had to do now was convince David of the viability of that move. And see Henry Campbell.

Chapter Four

It was the name of the little village of Bliss that drew Lila and Gordon to retire there in 1972. It appealed to Lila's romanticism. She just knew life there would be "blissful." Only it wasn't a village when they bought High Hope and moved there. Bliss consisted of a post office and a gas station—that was all.

Lila was further enamored with the Civil War history of the location. It was named after Robert Rutherford Bliss, a captain in the Confederate Army. A lot of people thought North Carolina had been on the side of the Union in the "war of Northern aggression," as it was called by some Southerners. When that opinion was expressed in Lila's presence, she was quick to correct the speaker. One of the East-West faces of a mountain had served as a kind of unofficial boundary between the North and South. No major battles took place in the area, but there were frequent skirmishes between the Southern Mountain Home Guard and Northern Yankee sympathizers. One of the most heated of those battles took place at

Bliss, where "good old Bob Bliss," as Lila called him, was successful in sending the sympathizers in a hasty retreat back to Tennessee.

Bliss was halfway between Boone, North Carolina, the Watauga County Seat, and Mountain City, Tennessee, about thirty minutes away in either direction. Boone, the home of Appalachian State University, was a charming mountain town that began to experience a growth explosion. Nearby Blowing Rock was populated mostly by wealthy retirees and second-home owners. Neither appealed to Lila and Gordon as much as Bliss, where there was nothing but a little history, a gorgeous old farm, and a lot of "high hopes" for the future.

After Lila got High Hope mostly the way she wanted it, though it would never be completely finished, she turned her attention to Bliss. After winning many arguments with Gordon and applying her irrepressibly persuasive abilities with retiring friends in Charlotte, she was single-handedly responsible for the creation of the village of Bliss as it existed when she died in 1999. The post office and gas station remained, of course, but in addition, little by little, the village grew to comprise a grocery store, which quickly became well known for its deli section and the wonderful sandwiches that could be consumed at the adjacent patio area; a drug store, which included an old-fashioned soda shop, a favorite of the youngsters in the area; three antique stores, one previously owned and operated by Lila and her friend Celia; a restaurant that served the best hamburgers in the county; a small community center with a library continually increasing in size and inventory; a hardware store and lumber yard out on the highway, along with a used car lot and garage; and—Gordon's favorite—an office building that housed the offices of a pediatrician, a dentist, and a general practitioner (who accepted no insurance, required payment in cash, and made house visits, when necessary). There was a dress shop and a few other small retail establishments. Gordon and Lila had owned the office building and held an interest in most of the other structures. Most of the proprietors and professionals were former friends from Charlotte, happy to get out of the city and live a slower-paced life in the mountains. Some were folks from Boone who were running satellite operations or were finding Boone's growth more hectic than they enjoyed. One of those was the lawyer Henry Campbell.

A hurricane had battered the North Carolina coast and moved inland toward the mountains, where it lost steam but brought lots of rain. It had been raining for two days and nights and was still raining when Winter and David arrived at High Hope after the funeral. The first thing Winter did upon arriving was light a fire in both fireplaces.

"A fire in July?" asked David, quizzically.

"Just to knock off the dampness," Winter replied.

"Uh huh. Right. It is damp. Chilly too," he said with a grin and a wink.

He had come to know many of Winter's idiosyncrasies, one of them being her love of a fire in the fireplace. She grinned back and went to the kitchen to heat the hot chocolate Ellen had left for them. Ellen knew Winter better than David had yet had the opportunity to know her. Ellen knew that a fire would immediately be lit, which is why both fireplaces had been loaded with firewood, and that a steaming cup of hot chocolate would be the next requirement. Flickering fires and hot chocolate just went together. It had been the same for Lila.

David and Winter snuggled together on the sofa, warmed by the fire, the hot chocolate, and each other. They sat quietly for a while, each in his or her own thoughts.

It was Winter who spoke first, her thoughts having been about how to approach David with her plan. She decided to ease into the subject.

"Comfy?"

"More than comfy. This is the most relaxed I have been since we were here last."

"Yeah, me, too. I guess we need to think about planning our party. When do you think we ought to have it?"

"Oh, I don't know. Fairly soon. How many people are you thinking of?"

"Actually, I was thinking of two parties. One on Saturday for everyone from Charlotte and elsewhere out of town, and a brunch on Sunday for everyone locally."

"The same weekend? That sounds like a lot."

"My thinking was to get it all over with. But we can break it up into two weekends, if you prefer?"

"That puts a burden on two weekends then. Why can't we have everybody all at once?"

"Well, because, for the most part, we are talking about two different kinds of people. For instance, what do Roy and your dad have in common? What would they talk about?"

"Yeah, I see what you mean. I don't care, honey. You plan it the way you want it. I'll show up. If you're good."

"Good? Good? I'll show you good, counselor."

The lovemaking that ensued, on the floor in front of the fire, was long, tender, and healing. It had been only six weeks since their lives had been torn apart by John's and Grace's deaths and the intense activity that followed. And while they had made love during that time, this time it seemed to mark the end of the tragedy they had endured together and a new beginning of the magic they found in each other.

Afterward, they lay in each other's arms while Winter sobbed softly. David didn't have to ask why she was crying. He blinked away a tear or two of his own. They were feeling the final moments of release from the pain of the last weeks. After a while, when they could smile at each other again, Winter sensed the right time to broach the subject of their move to High Hope.

"Honey?"

"Hmmm?"

"I want to ask you something."

"Do I have to answer?"

"Yes. The witness will answer the question."

"Okay. Okay. But not until we get some more hot chocolate."

Back on the sofa with fresh hot chocolate, they continued.

"Now, what is it you want to ask me?"

"I need to know how you feel about the people up here? The separate life I have—have always had—here?"

"That's two questions."

"Well, answer the first one first."

"How do I feel about the people up here? Well, let's see. Do you mean Ellen and Roy?"

"Yes, them, but all the others that you met when they came to Charlotte for the funeral. I know you had little more than an introduction with most of them. But I'm interested in your overall impression."

"You're getting at something. What is it?"

"Answer my question first."

"Well, they all seem to be quite nice. Salt of the earth

kind of people. Unsophisticated in some instances. Just plain uneducated in other instances. But all decent people nonetheless. Of course, the older friends of your grandparents who followed them up here, and your parents' contemporaries, don't fall into that category. They are not typical country or mountain folk. I liked all your friends from up here in different ways. Why?"

"What about the second question?"

"I forgot what it was."

"About your feelings about my life here?"

"What exactly do you mean by 'your life here'?"

"Well, you know. I have explained to you how much a part of me is always here in these mountains, in Bliss, in this house, with my grandmother, her things, her memory. How do you feel about that?"

David began to have a glimpse of where this conversation was headed. He was thoughtfully quiet for a moment, then said, "Can I have one more cup of hot chocolate before I answer?"

"I think there's more in the kitchen."

"Want another cup?"

"No, thanks, two is plenty for me."

David went to the kitchen, more for a few moments to ponder how to answer Winter's question and what he had begun to see the next question would be than for more hot chocolate. Winter waited, wondering what he was thinking, wondering if he had figured out what it was she really wanted to ask him. When he returned to the sofa, he went straight to the point.

"When were you thinking of moving up here?"

Oh, how she loved him in that moment, loved that direct, cut-to-the chase way he had of dealing with things. It gave her such a sense of freedom to know that, with her husband, her conversation was not required to be so heavily steeped in tact, diplomacy, and circuitousness, all of which were needed in large doses when, as a psychologist, she was dealing with her clients. She gave him a long, loving look before she answered.

"As soon as possible after we have decided this is the right move to make."

"What negative aspects about such a move have you identified?"

"I haven't thought of any. But then I recognize my bias. In terms of places, my heart is here. In terms of people, my heart is with you. We are sitting in High Hope. It is my highest hope that my love of you and this place can be realized together, at the same time."

"Baby, I think I'm going to need to think about this for just a little while."

"Well, sure. I knew you would want some time to chew on it. Why don't we just table the subject for a day or two?"

"I'll tell you what. You need to go see Henry Campbell tomorrow, don't you?"

"Yes."

"Okay. While you're gone, I'll take the time alone to analyze and consider it, and we'll go to dinner tomorrow night and talk about it some more then. How 'bout that?"

"Deal?"

"Deal."

"David?"

"What?"

"I love you."

"Really?"

Winter's response was a playful punch on David's arm and a long kiss of gratitude.

It wasn't long before watching TV produced yawns of boredom and sleepiness, and they went to bed curled up in the security and comfort of each other's arms.

Chapter Five

The next morning, Winter was awakened by the smell of the coffee Ellen had made. She heard Ellen stirring in the kitchen and eased out of bed to join her.

"Morning, Ellen," Winter said brightly, along with a hug and kiss on Ellen's forehead. "Why is the smell of coffee up here more wonderful than any place else in the world?"

"That's easy," replied Roy, who was just coming into the kitchen through the pantry door as Winter was greeting Ellen. "Because of Ellen's secret ingredient."

"What secret ingredient?" Winter asked. By the time Roy replied, he had come to Winter's side and was giving her a hug.

"Her love, sweet pea . . . her love." "Sweet pea" was Roy's pet name for Winter, and it warmed her heart every time Roy called her that.

"Well, you know, that just could be it," Winter said, smiling at Ellen. Winter poured her coffee and was suddenly overcome with love and gratitude for these two people who had helped raise her and loved her all her life. She had endured the loss of her grandmother and her parents, but at least she still had them. That was as much a comfort to her as her losses were painful.

"Roy, I've got to go see Henry Campbell today, and I thought while I was there, I'd take that load of stuff from Mom and Dad's next door to Miz Celia's and visit with her. Do you think you'll have time to drive the truck down there this afternoon? David can help you unload it."

"I can handle that, Sweet Pea. Just tell me when."

"Good. Thank you, Roy. My appointment with Henry is at two o'clock. I was thinking maybe David and I will go down for lunch, and if you could meet us at Miz Celia's about one, that would work out."

"I'll be there at one."

Miz Celia was the last of Lila and Gordon's friends whom Lila had talked into coming to Bliss to help make a town out of it. Miz Celia still ran the antique store she and Lila had owned together. Now Winter, having inherited the shop, was her partner.

"Winter, honey, was everything all right over here last night? I ask because at about two thirty this morning when I got up to go to the bathroom, I saw the living room lights on over here," Ellen asked.

"Lights on? Hmm. It wasn't me. I slept better than I have in a long time. If it was David, I didn't hear him. Two thirty? Hmm. No wonder he's still in bed at," glancing at the grandmother clock in the kitchen, "almost nine thirty. I think I'll go peek in on him."

"Do you want to wait for your French toast until later then? Do you think David will want French toast?"

"I'm sure he'll love your French toast. Who wouldn't? Yeah, I guess I'll wait for him. Let me go see if he's still sleeping."

Winter poured a fresh cup of coffee and eased into the master bedroom that had been her grandmother's. David looked to be still asleep. She started to sit down in her grandmother's rocking chair. But, as she looked at it and the nearby footstool, she thought about the innumerable times she had sat on the footstool, talking with her grandmother. They had talked about everything under the sun, from the time she was able to talk until a week before her death. Once again, Winter sat on that footstool, in reverie, sipping her coffee, watching the husband she felt so lucky to have found, looking around the room she knew so well—the paintings, family pictures, books, cherished gift items she had given to her grandmother. Being in that room, with that man, seemed to Winter to be what heaven must be like. She closed her eyes, called her grandmother to her mind, and remembered what she had told her about being married. "Let the criterion for whether or not you marry someone with whom you have fallen in love be whether or not you can commit to doing whatever it takes, short of subjecting yourself to abuse of any kind, to stay in the marriage and make it work, if in your heart you know, however hard it may sometimes be to stay married to that man, it would be even harder to live without him."

Winter had made that commitment to her marriage to David, but in her mind, she asked Lila, "But, Grandmother, what if 'whatever it takes' means giving up my dream of living at High Hope?" Winter let her mind be quiet, hoping to hear an answer from her grandmother. What she heard instead was David.

"I smell the coffee. All I have to do now is wake up."

"Well, it's about time, lazy bones," Winter replied as she sat on the bed next to him. "Here, drink this. It's just the right drinking temperature. I'll go get another cup."

When she returned, David was sitting up in bed, and she sat beside him. "Honey, were you up in the night?" she asked.

"Yes, did I disturb you?"

"No. I didn't even know it. I was deep in the sleep of the innocent, in the arms of Morpheus, as Grandmother used to call it. Ellen told me this morning that when she had been up to go to the bathroom, she had seen the living room lights on. What were you doing up at that hour? Couldn't sleep?"

Before David responded, he sat his coffee cup down, put Winter's hand to his lips, and kissed it long and tenderly. "I was wandering around in my new home, trying to see how it would feel, thinking what I might like to ask you to change to make it feel more like our home than your grandmother's. Like putting her clothes someplace else so that I can put my clothes in the closet."

Winter smiled that smile that could illuminate the darkest room; tears of joy sprang to her eyes. "Oh, David, really? Really? Oh, yes, darling, we can change whatever you like. Oh, thank you, thank you. I love you so much." She began showering his face with kisses. "Let me go tell Roy and Ellen. They'll be so thrilled."

"Hold on. Wait a minute, now. Before we start making announcements, there are some things that need to be worked out. I was thinking, for instance, that when you go to see Henry today, when you're through with your business, I'll spend a little time with him to explore the possibility of practicing with him, in Bliss, in Boone, or wherever. I'd just like to get some advice from him. Then, we'll know better about the timing of a move. Don't forget that I have open cases in Charlotte that would need to be resolved. Don't forget your obligations to clients in Charlotte as well."

"Okay, I'll wait until we've made those decisions.

The big one has been made, though, right? It's only a matter of timing, right?"

"Right, honey. We're coming home to the mountains. I couldn't stand in the way of that dream of yours, and by the way, I feel very drawn toward getting out of Dodge, myself. Let's just take our time and plan it properly. For instance, do you think you would want your practice to be up here? If so, where? In Boone? In Bliss? Your own practice or in association with another psychologist?"

"See, I've already made my decisions, in my dream, my Winter-time dream. Yes, I want to practice here. I want to open an office right next to yours, wherever you decide that is to be. But I hope it is in Bliss. And I want our offices to have an adjoining door, so that when the baby is born, when I have a client in, you can look after him—her, it—and vice versa when you have a client."

"What baby? Are you trying to tell me something?"

"The baby, my darling, that, unless my period is two weeks late for some other reason, and unless the funky feeling I have been having in the mornings is being caused by something else, is, as we speak, growing in my belly."

"Winter! Honey! My God! Why didn't you tell me?"

"I am telling you. Now. But I probably shouldn't be until we do the test. But what else could it be? I'm as regular as clockwork. Are you happy?"

"Aw, baby, happy isn't the word for it. I'm thrilled. I'm ecstatic. Let's go right now and get a test kit to confirm it."

"Whoa, now you're the one who needs to slow down. Ellen is making us her fabulous French toast. Then, later, we'll go into town, go to the drugstore, get the test, have lunch, and I'll go see Henry while you and Roy unload that truck full of stuff at Miz Celia's, then you can visit with Henry and I'll go home and do the test. Okay?"

"Okay. Then we'll go to—what's the name of your favorite restaurant in Blowing Rock?"

"Manor Cellar."

"Right. We'll go there and talk about all this some more."

"Okay, good. But I don't think I can hide my excitement from Roy and Ellen. Can I tell them we're coming, don't know when, but we're coming? Please?"

"Oh, all right. Yes, go tell them and let me get a shower."

After one more shower of kisses on David's face, and a pop on her behind from David as she tore off hollering for Ellen and Roy, David took himself and his thoughts to the shower. A new marriage. A new home. A new practice. The loss of his in-laws. The probability that his wife is pregnant. "Wow," he thought to himself, "that's a hell of a lot to absorb in a short period of time." If only David had known what more was to come.

Chapter Six

After having met with Henry Campbell while Winter had gone to the drugstore, then to home, David headed toward High Hope. As he started up the driveway, he heard loud music that he recognized as Beethoven's Fifth Symphony blasting from inside the house. He sat in the car for a moment after parking, having been reminded of a Lila story Winter had told him.

As a little girl, Winter was very afraid of storms and the winter winds, which could be ferocious. On one particularly windy night, in the wee hours of the morning, Winter crept into Lila's room to crawl into her bed. Lila hadn't been sound asleep because of the wind, which would shake the house with its gusts and which she knew was frightening Winter. Lila knew Winter would soon need to be in bed with her.

"Are you letting that big old wind scare you, honey?" Lila asked Winter.

"Yes, ma'am. I don't like it. It scares me. Makes me

afraid the house is going to fall down when it blows so hard and loud."

"You know what?" said Lila. "I may have a solution for this problem. Come with me to the living room."

So they both went to the living room, where Lila put Beethoven's Fifth on an old record player and cranked the volume up almost to full strength. It was loud and angry sounding. During World War II, the Allies wanted a piece to use in their propaganda to support the war effort. The Fifth Symphony stood out because, in addition to being awesome, that famous opening, repeated throughout—the *da da da dummm*—put in Morse code, short short short long, is the letter *V*, a popular Allied slogan of *V* for victory.

Lila told Winter that the wind was only the song of winter and that when the wind frightened her, she should roar back at it with Beethoven's Fifth Symphony, and for any time she was really scared about anything. "Let the energy of this music eat up and overwhelm your scary feelings."

About that time, John and Grace came bounding downstairs, yelling, "What in the world is going on down here?" "Oh," replied Lila, "she didn't like winter's song, so we're roaring back at the wind with our own loud song." John and Grace gaped at Lila and Winter before John spoke. "For God's sake, Mother, you two shut off that noise and go back to bed!" Which they did, but not before they grinned and winked at each other.

No storm was raging or wind blowing, so, remembering what Lila had told Winter, he became anxious about what scary feeling Winter was trying to overwhelm with the loud music. He hurried into the house, calling for Winter. He finally found her sitting on the floor of her grandmother's closet, clutching an old, worn-out, blue chenille robe that had been Lila's favorite and a piece of paper, which she thrust toward David with a shaking hand. It was a letter that Henry had given her—from Lila. David calmed Winter and helped her up and out of the closet. They went to the sofa in the living room, where David held her, shaking and still clutching the robe. After a few minutes, Winter finally calmed down enough to allow David to read the letter and learn what had so frightened his Winter.

The letter read,

My darling Winter,

If you are reading this, it means that John and Grace are dead and buried. Obviously, I can't know how old you are at the time you are reading this, or what the circumstances of your life may be. I can only hope that you are sufficiently mature to absorb and understand what I am about to tell you, and that you

*have love relationships in your life that will support
you and help you through what I'm sure will impact
you strongly.*

*You are to get in touch with Susan right away, if
she is still alive by the time you are reading this, or
her surrogate. As you have learned from Tom and
a review of my will, I have left Susan an extremely
large trust fund. Those funds, and the reason for the
bequest, are for the purpose of maintaining me in a
different kind of life. Winter, if all has gone well with
what Susan and I have agreed to pursue, I am not
dead at all.*

*After meeting with Susan or her surrogate, you
will understand why I have allowed you and the family
to believe that I had died. You will immediately think
how cruel it was of me to do that. As I said, when you
find out the circumstances, you'll understand.*

*Contact Susan or whomever at 912-555-2300.
Yes, that's a North Carolina area code. That's where
I am—in North Carolina. Just call and make an
appointment to come visit. All will be made clear to
you.*

I love you so much, as I always have.

Grandmother

David, after having read the letter twice, put it
down and looked at Winter. She had stopped crying

but was staring off into space in a daze. He put his arm around her and pulled her close, waiting a few minutes before he spoke.

"Wow! No wonder you are all undone. When do you think you want to make that call?"

"I don't know, honey. Not today. I need a little time to get my head around this and prepare myself for whatever it will be that is ahead of me."

"I think that's a very good decision. Maybe it would help to put it in the back of your mind for right now and turn your attention to what we had planned for today. There is a super important question for which we can find an answer in a few minutes."

Winter looked at him quizzically, then it dawned on her. "The pregnancy test!" Up she jumped to run to her purse, then to the bathroom. When she returned, she was crying again, only this time tears of joy. She was, in fact, pregnant with David's child. He could barely contain his joy and excitement, but not wanting to be insensitive to her having been so distraught just moments ago.

It was about that time that Roy and Ellen returned from having gone to town. As Winter started toward them, she whispered to David, "Not a word about the letter." Then, to the Shandses, "Roy, Ellen, come sit with us a moment. We have news."

Ellen set the bags on the counter, and she and Roy

joined Winter and David in the living room. "What news?" asked Ellen.

"Well," Winter began, "remember I told you that David and I have decided to live here at High Hope permanently?"

Roy spoke next, again trying to hide his emotions. "We had hoped, and yes, we had prayed, that you would decide to do that. That makes us both so happy." At that point, Roy could no longer control his quivering lip, so he stopped talking.

"David, what about your practice in Charlotte. And yours, Winter?" Ellen asked.

"There are lots of details to be worked out, and we have already begun the first steps of making arrangements, and obviously there will be some changes made here. But, Ellen, Roy, there's more."

"What else, Winter?"

"We're all going to be raising a baby in this house. I'm pregnant."

That was it. While Roy and Ellen had held back from rushing to Winter and David with hugs about the news of their living at High Hope, with this news, there was no holding back. Ellen was crying and Roy unabashedly joined her as they went to Winter and David to embrace them. Winter and David stood to receive the demonstration of their joy, and the four of them stood silently together, hugging, holding hands, or just touching. It was one of those moments in life that makes so much of the grief experienced along the way bearable.

Ellen broke the silence. "Well, Roy, we better get these groceries put away. There's ice cream in one of those bags." And off they went to the kitchen, chattering about what they had just learned.

David took Winter into his arms and gently kissed her. Then he asked if she felt like going to dinner, as they had planned. He had a lot to tell her, too. She agreed to go and left to get dressed.

Chapter Seven

Manor Cellar had been a large cabin residence tucked into the woods on a hillside before being converted into a restaurant. John and Grace had loved to take guests there to have them wonder where in the world they were going as they were taken high up a long, narrow gravel driveway—a pig trail, John loved to call it. Once inside, they understood. In cold weather the fireplace welcomed customers to a beautiful, rustic interior where at all times of the year, award-winning cuisine was served.

Winter and David were greeted by the manager with a hug and words of condolence then ushered to the Lassiter table. Winter, and any of the Lassiters for that matter, had a table reserved for them and not to be used by anyone else unless and until there were no other tables available and the manager had checked to see if one of the Lassiters might be needing it, because John Gordon and Lila, with some investor friends, owned Manor Cellar. The land at the back of the restaurant was very steep and came to a small creek at the bottom. John had wanted to put a miniature dock and boats in the creek, light it, and call the restaurant the Blowing Rock Yacht Club, but Lila overruled him. So it was named the Manor Cellar.

The origin of the "Blowing Rock" name was based on a legend. A huge boulder stuck out into the air from the side of one of the mountains. It was told that a young Indian girl and an Indian boy from another tribe fell in love but were forbidden to marry. In desolation, the girl jumped from the boulder, but the wind blew up from the land far below so hard that she was blown back up into her lover's arms. The "blowing rock" had been developed into a tourist trap where visitors could see the boulder that jutted out into space and toss a tissue out to see if it would get blown back up. Most times, it did.

John was shot down with his idea for naming the restaurant the Blowing Rock Yacht Club, but when he and some investors developed an eighteen-hole golf course, they all agreed that it should be named Puffin' Pebble, and what a golf course it was. One green was almost eight feet below the tee. Fortunately, the fairway had been made extra wide and long so that when the ball was struck into space, it had a chance of landing on the fairway. One green had been carved out of the side of a rocky hill. The green was almost surrounded on three sides by a stone wall. If golfers overshot the green, the ball would hit the stone wall and bounce back somewhere onto the green. One golfer declared that the Puffin' Pebble golf course was actually goofy golf, but everyone, it seemed, enjoyed the challenge of playing the course.

After settling in with a cocktail for David and a soft drink for Winter, it was David who began the conversation with his meeting with Henry Campbell. Henry Campbell was a large, pear-shaped man with huge hands and a brusque manner about him. The way in which he answered the phone was not "hello," not "yes," not "Henry Campbell"; he answered the phone by gruffly saying "Aaawwright." He answered a call in that way while David was there. The call was from his secretary, Clara, to tell him that his next appointment had arrived. Having almost concluded their conversation about the prospect of David practicing law in a new office in Bliss, Henry asked David to stay to meet the waiting client and sit in on their conference. David thought this odd, but agreed.

The client ushered in was Tommy Lee Higgins, a young backwoods mountain man. After introducing David to Tommy Lee and explaining that it might be David who would be handling his case, Henry asked what he could do for him.

Tommy Lee told the story of his having married Patsy Blair six months before. The marriage did not go well, and Patsy went back home to her mother and filed for divorce. The only asset owned by both Patsy and Tommy Lee was a mobile home they had purchased shortly after their wedding. In the divorce decree it was ordered that this asset be split equally between them. Tommy Lee interpreted this literally and, with a chainsaw, cut the mobile home in half, explaining, "I gave her the half with the kitchen fer I don't know how ta cook." At her mother's urging, Patsy went back to her divorce lawyer, who referred the case to the district attorney, who filed suit against Tommy Lee for destruction of jointly owned property and demanded replacement of the mobile home with one that was whole. Failure to do so, Tommy Lee was told, would result in his being charged with destruction of jointly owned property, which carried a penalty of a maximum of two years in the county jail. Not having the money to replace the mobile home and having previously been sentenced to jail on another charge, Tommy Lee was terrified about the possibility of having to go back to jail. He needed Henry to help him avoid that outcome.

David listened to this sad tale of woe with his mouth agape. When Tommy Lee finished telling his story, Henry responded by telling him that he needn't worry because he felt sure that he and David, whom he introduced as an associate, together could keep him out of jail, and that he would be in touch. Tommy Lee breathed a sigh of relief, thanked Henry, and left. Henry then looked at David and told him this was an example of some of the kinds of cases he would be handling, should he decide to practice law in Bliss. That example saved Henry thousands of words trying to explain the nature of some of the people in the region and some of the cases that would be brought to him. He advised David to think long and hard about practicing with him in Bliss.

It took David the time to consume two drinks while Winter sipped ginger ale to convey to Winter how his meeting with Henry had gone. "So how do you feel about it?" Winter asked.

"At first, I was sort of stunned by the lack of education of Tommy Lee. I've defended some real characters in Charlotte, but I can't think of any case like this. Then I realized that Tommy Lee and others like him in Watauga County were the most in need of legal counsel."

"So does that mean you're going to practice with Henry in Bliss? Are you thinking of the two of you practicing in a new building?"

"Yes, honey, I think it's going to be very interesting and make a fabulous book one day."

Winter reached for David's hand with a smile on her face just as the waiter came to take their dinner order. When the waiter left, Winter asked, "So how did Henry say he could get Tommy Lee out of that mess?"

"Oh," David responded, "he said something about his long relationship with the judge and wanted me to go with him to meet the judge, if I decided to stay on with him."

Winter asked, "So did you tell him you would practice with him?"

"Yes," said David, "and he seemed pleased about that. We talked about office space until we could get a building of our own built, which would be no problem, as he already had a spare office on his premises in Boone. We talked about scheduling, and he told me he would let me know about when I would need to be here to meet the judge and see what we could do for Tommy Lee."

Over an after-dinner drink and dessert for Winter, David asked, "So, are you ready to talk about your grandmother's letter?"

"Oh, David, I don't know. My mind has been swirling with questions. We were told that she had died in California, that she had donated her body to science and that there were complications about getting her body back here for burial, so Susan had her laid to rest there. Now, the letter says she is in North Carolina. Where in North Carolina? When and how was her body brought here? Why were we not told? What does she mean by 'I'm not really dead'? What could that possibly mean? If she were alive, she would be 101 by now. Susan was a classmate, so that means she would be 101 as well. When I think about making that call, a feeling of dread comes over me. I'm not sure why, but there's resistance. With so much going on in our lives, I think I'll just put that on the back burner temporarily."

"I'm so glad to hear you say that, and I couldn't agree more. I don't want any more stress on you than is absolutely necessary so that you can enjoy your pregnancy and the baby will develop in a happy place."

They both returned to Charlotte the next day to begin the process of closing down their practices. Ellen was asked to get all of Lila's clothes out of the closet at High Hope. What would have been really hard for Ellen to do was now done cheerfully when she considered the reason for it. Her precious Winter, David, and their baby would be living here. What joy!

Meanwhile, Winter contacted Ellen and Roy's son, Christopher Shands, to talk about building offices for them and Henry with a nursery in between and an apartment above intended to be used as a residence for a nanny on call, when needed. Christopher was overjoyed about the news that Winter and David would be living in Bliss and excited about building their offices on a piece of property Winter had inherited. It was one street behind the highway and high enough to give them a pretty mountain view. It was not like the view from High Hope, where the mountain peaks in three states, North Carolina, Tennessee, and Virginia, could be seen, with mountains rippling one ridge after another across the sky. But it was a pretty view nonetheless.

The Appalachian Mountains, argue some, are the second oldest on the planet, given when and how they were formed and geologic discoveries. Over the eons, wind and rain had softened the mountain peaks, allowing for seeds of all kinds to take root and grow. Unlike younger mountain ranges, such as the western Rockies, the Appalachian Mountains were lush and green with trees and shrubbery of all kinds. There was not an Appalachian Mountain view that was not pretty in North Carolina or the adjoining states.

During the next month, Winter and David came to High Hope every weekend, bringing with each trip things from their apartment to be included among the furnishings of High Hope and making changes that would help David feel like it was their home instead of Lila's. At one point, David turned his attention to the portrait of Lila in the living room. Winter noticed him standing and staring at it and went to his side. About that time, Ellen came into the room, saw them both standing and staring, and joined them. There the three of them stood, staring at the portrait of Lila, with David wondering if he dared ask that it be removed. Winter was a step ahead of him. "Maybe," she said, "the best place for Grandmother's portrait would be in my new office." David looked at her and took her in his arms. No words needed to be spoken for Winter to express her love for David in this way, nor for David's gratitude for that expression. Their hearts knew.

Chapter Eight

Henry Campbell had arranged for David and Judge Earl Stanley to meet for lunch on one of the Saturdays David would be in town. After pleasantries, Henry broached the subject of Tommy Lee and his problem. Judge Stanley laughed uproariously at the part where Tommy Lee cut the trailer in half. Judge Stanley knew these mountain folk and some of the unusual cases over which he had presided, but this one took the cake. "Well," he said, "we'll see what we can do for poor old Tommy Lee." And with that, the subject was dropped until a hearing date had been established, after Tommy Lee had been arraigned and released on his own recognizance.

When David arrived at the courthouse for the hearing that had been scheduled for Tommy Lee, he was startled by the presence of a judge other than Judge Stanley. It seems Judge Stanley had taken ill and a traveling circuit judge had filled in for him. David was taken aback by this eventuality, especially since Henry

Campbell had a conflicting court appearance in a neighboring county, leaving David to deal with Tommy Lee's case on his own. David pled not guilty to the charge against Tommy Lee of the destruction of jointly owned property by reason of the uneducated Tommy Lee having misinterpreted the wording of the divorce decree, and therefore David had filed a motion for the case to be dismissed. Judge Stanley, having full knowledge of the plaintiff and the circumstances, would presumably have ordered a psychological evaluation of Tommy Lee, by Winter, of course, and ultimately accepted David's plea, and the matter would be over. The district attorney responded to David's defense of Tommy Lee's action by stating that misinterpretation was not a reasonable defense because Tommy Lee should have consulted with someone who could have explained the meaning of the lawsuit. David retorted that Tommy Lee didn't know that he was misinterpreting the wording of the lawsuit or that he needed any kind of help with it.

After sitting for what seemed an especially long time just staring at Tommy Lee in disbelief that anyone could be that stupid, the judge denied David's motion and ordered that Tommy Lee be bound over for trial with bail set at ten thousand dollars. When Tommy Lee was handcuffed and escorted to the county jail, his look toward David was one of mixed terror and rage.

The trial date was set for three weeks hence.

It took two weeks for Tommy Lee's family and friends to gather the one thousand dollars needed for the bail bond. When he was released, he headed directly to the half of the mobile home he had kept, with the bedroom, the bathroom, and what had been the back door. He had boarded up the missing wall where the rest of the mobile home had been attached to provide shelter for himself. It was there that he kept his belongings, including his shotgun.

David met with Henry Campbell immediately after his return to the office to discuss Tommy Lee's case. David suggested that Winter evaluate Tommy Lee's mental health. That evaluation, to be sure, would provide evidence that Tommy Lee's mental capacity was such that he would have been incapable of correctly interpreting the wording of the divorce decree or even of being aware that he was misinterpreting it. Henry agreed that this would be a good strategy and expressed his strong regret that he had not been able to be with David for the hearing. He would, however, be there for Tommy Lee's trial.

After David discussed the matter with Winter, she and he went to the jail before Tommy Lee was bailed out to meet with him and explain how and why the hearing had turned out the way it did and what would be taking place next.

Tommy Lee was brought to the room provided for consultation with counsel. He was wide-eyed and shaking so intensely that he could barely walk. He struggled into a seat across from Winter and David. David began to introduce Winter, but before he could utter even a few words, Tommy Lee interrupted him.

"There's a bad man here," he said.

"What bad man?" asked David.

"A bad man."

"Why is he a bad man?"

"He hurt me."

"How did he hurt you, Tommy Lee?"

"He done what a man's s'posed to do with a woman . . . not a man."

Winter and David looked at each other, understanding that Tommy Lee had been raped.

"Tommy Lee, could you show us the bad man? Was he a guard or one of the inmates—one of the other men here in jail?"

"He's a bad man."

"Yes, Tommy Lee, we're sure he is, and we'd like to know who that bad man is so that he can be punished for hurting you."

"Can't tell who he is. He'll hurt me again."

David assured Tommy Lee they wouldn't let that happen. "Tommy Lee, we're going to talk to the boss of this jail—the man who is in charge—and make sure you won't be hurt again, but we need to know who the bad man is."

"Why did you make me come here so that bad man could hurt me? Mr. Campbell said I woodun' have to come here again."

David tried to explain, in the simplest way he could, about he and Henry having already talked to Judge Stanley, who was supposed to have been the judge that day, so that the judge would understand Tommy Lee's situation even before they went to court. He explained that Judge Stanley had become ill and couldn't be in court that day. The new judge didn't know Tommy Lee and didn't know what the circumstances were. David hesitated before going into who Winter was, why she was there, and what would be happening next. By Tommy Lee's response to David's attempt at an explanation, it was clear that the information had not registered in Tommy Lee's mind.

"You made me come to this bad place and that bad man hurt me."

Winter spoke up at that point. "Tommy Lee, my name is Winter. Would it be okay if you and I talked for a little while? I'd like to get to know you. I think I can help when you have to go to court again."

Tommy Lee looked long and hard at Winter, then asked, "Can you take me home now?"

"No, Tommy Lee. I wish I could, but I can't. You're

going to have to stay here for a little while longer. But we're going to make sure no one is going to hurt you again while you're here."

Tommy Lee glared at David with pure hatred in his eyes, got up, went to the door and opened it, stepped into the hall where a guard was waiting, and disappeared with him. David and Winter went immediately to Sheriff Red Potter to apprise him of what had happened to Tommy Lee in his jail and to ask him to take measures to ensure he would be safe for the remainder of the time he was there. Red was already aware of what had happened. One of the other inmates found out about it and brought it to the attention of one of the guards. Turned out it had been another guard who had raped Tommy Lee, and he had already been fired and charged with rape; he was now himself an inmate of the jail, in solitary confinement for his own safety. Tommy Lee wouldn't be bothered by that "bad man" again.

As David and Winter drove home, David asked, "Well, what do you think?"

"I doubt he has an IQ over 60," she said. "I don't know how he has managed to get along in life this far, much less get married. In my own preliminary opinion, he needs to be institutionalized for a while for therapy and some basic education. Do you think he ever went to school?"

"I don't know. I'll ask Henry. I think he knows the family. It's obvious that if he did go to school, it wasn't for very long. Henry's back in his office, so I think I'll go back into town and talk to him about this mess."

On the way home, they stopped by the site of their new office building and met with Christopher. He was doing a wonderful job on the building and seemed overly anxious to please David and Winter. It was coming right along and would be finished in just a few weeks. Little did they know then that they would never be moving into those offices together.

Chapter Nine

By all rights, Boone, North Carolina, shouldn't even have been there. Before the Revolutionary War, an agreement was reached between the British government and the Cherokee Indians that no settlers would go beyond the Appalachian Mountains. That agreement was not honored by the immigrants who were coming to the colonies by the thousands: the Scotch-Irish, Germans, Dutch. When they settled the village of Boone, they had sense enough to establish it higher than the Happy Valley that lay between mountain ranges that had continued to become developed over the years. The original Boone was called "Old Boone" or downtown Boone. The Happy Valley wasn't very happy in 1940, when successive storms dumped more water on the mountains than they could absorb, and it all flowed down the mountains, bringing the myriad rivers and creeks beyond their capacity and causing a dam to break, completely flooding Boone. Although there hadn't been a flood of that magnitude since, with heavy rains, Winkler's Creek frequently rose above its banks to flood the shopping center parking lot, and warnings abounded of flash floods from the many creeks flowing down from the mountains.

Three months had passed since the deaths of John and Grace, Winter and David's wedding and their decision to move to Bliss, Winter becoming pregnant, and the activities pertaining to these events. It was almost "leaf season," when the changing colors of the leaves brought visitors to the mountains to take in the glorious yellow, orange, and red, clogging up the roads, filling up all the hotels, and causing an increase in the number of auto accidents and calls for the fire department because of "leafers" looking at the leaves rather than the road.

Henry Campbell's office was in Old Boone, where Appalachian State University was located. His office building was right next to a fire station. Henry's secretary, Clara, was on the phone with her back turned toward the door, rifling through a file cabinet drawer, so she didn't see Tommy Lee come into the office with his shotgun. At the same moment that a fire engine started out of the station with its siren on, Tommy Lee aimed his shotgun at Henry, said, "You let them take me to jail when you told me they wouldn't," and fired into Henry's chest. Because the siren from next door was blaring, neither Clara nor David in the adjoining office heard the shot. David's door was open. Tommy

Lee then saw David sitting at his desk and went into his office. "You let a bad man hurt me," he said, and fired his shotgun into David's chest. By that time, the wailing of the siren had begun to wane, so that Clara thought she heard something that sounded like a gunshot and looked toward the front door, thinking it had come from outside. She was sitting there looking and listening when Tommy Lee came into the front of the office, shotgun in hand. She looked at him, recognizing then that the gunshot she thought she had heard had come from inside the office, and asked, "Oh, Tommy Lee, what have you done? What in the name of God have you done?"

"I done kilt Mr. Henry and that David feller. They lied to me 'bout goin' to jail."

Clara gasped and began to cry. Through her tears, she said, "Oh, Lord, no! Tommy Lee, don't you know you will be going to jail for the rest of your life for doing this?" The reality of that statement came crashing into his mind, Tommy Lee not having thought of the consequences of his actions before. Now he knew that what she had said was true. He put the shotgun in his mouth and pulled the trigger. Clara screamed, reached for the phone, and dialed 911. Then she went to the doorway of Henry's office. She muffled her scream with her hand and hastily turned away.

Two ambulances arrived in just a few minutes,

along with the Boone police and Sheriff Red Potter, but it was too late for either Henry or David to be saved. Their wounds were fatal. Sheriff Potter went to Clara, who was huddled in a corner shaking and crying hysterically. He took her into his arms, held her and cried with her, in sympathy for what she had just endured and for himself, knowing that he would have to bring this horror to Winter.

Red pulled into the driveway at High Hope but couldn't make himself get out of the car right away. He sat there, bracing himself for what he had to do.

Ellen was in the kitchen cooking dinner, and Winter had just poured herself a cup of tea and walked to the window, as she frequently did, to see if the view of the mountains was clear that day and the cows were grazing in the pasture. When she saw Sheriff Potter's cruiser in the driveway, she went outside to the deck and waved to him. She saw his car door open and then his hesitant exit from the car. He looked up at Winter, and he couldn't help it—tears started smarting in his eyes. As he approached Winter, she knew he was bringing more bad news to her. "Winter," he said, "there's no good way to tell you this. Tommy Lee Higgins went to Henry Campbell's office and shot him and David, then himself. Winter, they're all dead." Winter dropped her freshly made tea and passed out cold. The sheriff caught her and called for Ellen. Winter had left the door to the deck open, and Ellen, having heard the teacup fall and break, went to investigate just as the sheriff was picking Winter up. He took her to the bedroom that he had known to be Lila's and laid her on the bed. Ellen went to the bedside, shouting, "Winter! Winter! Sheriff, what's happened to her?" He told Ellen that Winter was okay, and then he had to repeat the terrible news that had caused Winter to faint. Ellen fell to her knees and threw herself across Winter, crying uncontrollably, as though she wanted to protect her from what was to come: grief beyond description.

Winter came to after a few minutes. She stroked Ellen's head lying on her chest and said, "Ellen . . . ?" Then she looked up at Sheriff Potter, and what he had just told her fell in on her mind and heart. "No! No! No!" she screamed, moving Ellen away and getting out of the bed. She wandered around the house, her hands clutching her hair at her temples, and continued to wail and scream. Finally, she fell onto the sofa and was able to ask Sheriff Potter, "Where is he? Where is David?" The sheriff replied that he was no doubt in the morgue at the hospital. "I want to see him," she sobbed. "I've got to go see him." Sheriff Potter took her arm as she was headed toward the back door and said, "Honey, you're in no condition to drive. I'll take you." Ellen spoke up to say, "I'll go, too."

Sheriff Potter took them to the exterior door that

led directly to the morgue and pressed the button to let someone inside know he was requesting entry. In a moment or two, a doctor came to the door and ushered them in. "She's come to see her husband, David Thorpe."

"Well," the doctor said, "he hasn't been prepared for viewing yet."

"I don't care," screamed Winter. "Let me see him. Let me see him. Where is he?"

Sheriff Potter said a word or two to the doctor, and Winter and Ellen were told to wait there in the entryway for a few minutes. Finally, the doctor came and escorted Winter, Ellen, and Sheriff Potter to a room where David's body had been brought and covered with a sheet, except for his head. As Winter approached David, then stood beside him, she was weak and trembling. Ellen and Sheriff Potter both put their arms around her for fear she would faint again. Winter didn't faint. She stroked David's hair and kissed his forehead again and again. Then, suddenly, she put her hands to her stomach, remembering that she was pregnant, pregnant with David's baby. She knew she had to calm down, that David would want her to calm down so as not to bring harm to the baby, and so she did. She calmed down and quietly asked Sheriff Potter if he would take her and Ellen home, which, of course, he did.

Roy had been at a friend's place to help out with

repairing a fence and had not been there for all these events. When he returned home, he found Ellen and Winter sitting in the living room on the sofa, sobbing. Ellen responded to his questions by telling him what had happened. Roy went to Winter, sat down beside her, and pulled her to him. Together, they cried and cried.

Finally, they had cried all the tears they could. All of a sudden, Winter jumped up and ran to the desk in her bedroom. She had put Lila's mysterious letter there. Suddenly, she wanted her grandmother, no matter whether she was dead or alive. She had to find her grandmother and be with her. She picked the letter up, then put it back in the drawer. The feeling of dread had come over her again.

There were other things to attend to before she could turn her attention to the letter and her grand-mother. First, of course, she had to inform David's parents about what had happened. She called his father at his office first, so that he could absorb the news and make himself ready to tell David's mother in person. Then, there were all the things one must do in such circumstances: a newspaper obituary, choosing a casket and a set of burial clothes, and making arrangements for what was to be done with the body.

David and Winter had already firmly established that when one of them died, he or she was to be cremated and the ashes preserved until the other had died and been cremated; then their ashes were to be mixed and half of them scattered at High Hope, the other half given to David's parents for whatever they wished to do with them. David had said he knew he would be nearest to Winter with half of his ashes scattered there at the place that was so much a part of her. There was only one problem: they had not yet informed the Thorpes of that decision. David's parents had purchased a plot in the Thorpe family cemetery for him years ago. To their credit, after having been told of David's wishes in the matter and taking a little time to think about it, they acquiesced to the cremation plan. Also, they agreed on two services, one in Charlotte and another memorial service in Boone. All those arrangements had to be made.

Finally, everything was over. Nothing more to be taken care of. Her half of the ashes would be delivered to her in a couple of days. Back home at High Hope, she was lost. She didn't know who she was anymore. She didn't have a tomorrow and didn't want to think about the yesterdays. It was as though she suddenly had no plans, no dreams, no life. It was all gone with David. Her grandmother leaped into her mind with a phrase Winter had heard her say in jest so many times whenever something difficult arose: "Booze is the only answer." Winter managed half a grin at the memory, then thought, "No, Grandmother, not this time. Although it may help me get some sleep." With that, she poured herself a stiff drink and sat in the rocking chair on the front deck, waiting for darkness to fall and the stars to start the twinkling that could only be seen out in the country, with no city lights. She poured another drink, then another, from which she took only a sip before stumbling to bed, where she plopped, clothes and all. There she slept long and hard for the first time in many days.

On the next morning, she awoke to the smell of bacon frying. Ellen was in the kitchen cooking, as always. The ordinary routine felt good to Winter. Everything had been so bizarre during the past several days. She went to the kitchen, hugged Ellen, poured a cup of coffee, and sat down at the kitchen table with her head in her hands. Ellen noticed that she was still in the clothes she had worn the day before but didn't mention it. Intuitively, she knew that Winter didn't need conversation but rather peace and quiet for her soul to begin to heal.

Roy came in from the barn, saw Winter, got coffee for himself, and sat down at the table. "Leaves are colorin' up early this year," he said, trying to behave normally. Winter managed a weak smile to acknowledge that he had spoken. Ellen looked at him and shook her head no. After a few minutes, she asked Winter if she wanted eggs or waffles for breakfast. "Neither," she replied, "just some toast and jelly and maybe some bacon." Breakfast was consumed silently, Winter not wanting to speak and Roy and Ellen afraid to do so.

A knock at the door announced the arrival of Christopher Shands. Ellen brought him in and asked if he had had breakfast. He said he had and turned to Winter. "Winter, I thought I'd stop by to see if you have had a minute to think about what to do with the offices." Winter had not given a single thought to the offices but now needed to decide what to do about them. After a moment or two, she told Christopher to go ahead and finish them. They were already more than halfway done. She would decide later what to do with them, once they were finished. He thanked her and quickly left. Being in the presence of such pain was most uncomfortable for him.

Winter went to her bedroom, where she couldn't stop the tears from flowing again. The offices. Oh, what beautiful plans they had made! How exciting it had been to make plans for the baby. The baby! "Oh, my God," she thought. "What have I done to the baby with all that booze I drank last night?" Immediately, she called her doctor to ask what harm she might have done to the baby. He reassured her that probably there had been no harm with this single incident but that, of course, she should abstain from alcohol until she gave birth. She tried to feel okay about it after that conversation and headed to the bathroom for a long, hot shower. She thought maybe that would help clear her head, so she'd be capable of thinking about what should come next.

It had taken the fifteen-year-old Winter several weeks to begin to adjust to the fact that her grandmother was gone. That process interfered with her education, and she'd had to go to summer school to get back on schedule. Meanwhile, she pressured her parents to go to High Hope every weekend, and when they refused from time to time, she begged for a bus ticket so that she could go alone. Ellen and Roy would pick her up on Friday night and take her back to the bus station on Sunday night.

While she was at High Hope, she slept in her grandmother's bed, wore her grandmother's nightgowns or pajamas, and spent long hours just sitting in her grandmother's rocking chair, frequently just sitting and sobbing. Ellen and Roy let her be in the beginning but then did their best to get her out of that room and participating in some activity with them. There were the flower and vegetable gardens to tend. Winter resisted doing even that until Ellen finally told her that this is what she and her grandmother used to do together, that this is what her grandmother would want her to continue to do, and besides, Roy could use the help. Hearing that, Winter acquiesced, but it would be a very long time before she could smile or laugh at Roy's attempts at humor.

Now, here she was, a thirty-two-year-old pregnant widow, feeling much the same way as when her grandmother had died—lost, grief-stricken beyond what words could express, trying to figure out how to live the rest of her life.

The first thing that popped into her mind was making that phone call about her grandmother. Despite all the mystery, she so hoped that she would learn something about her grandmother that would help her through the pain she was experiencing. She knew that had her grandmother been here, she would have known just what to say, just what to do, other than making reference to booze, to help Winter through this horrible ordeal. She never could have guessed what she was about to learn about her grandmother.

Unbeknownst to Winter, after she had jumped up, when she had learned of David's death, to run to her desk and look at some kind of paper, Ellen later became curious and found the letter from Lila in the desk. After she had gotten over the shock of that letter, she spoke not a word of it to anyone, not even to Roy. She waited. She just waited. She knew Winter would make that call one day, and whatever she learned would be yet another trauma for her, so she waited, knowing how much Winter would need her when that occurred.

Chapter Ten

All the grief and sorrow Winter had experienced through all the tragedies of the previous year were completely overcome with the joy of the birth of her son, David Earle Thorpe Jr., that spring. Of course, Ellen and Roy were with her for the birth, such a comfort in the absence of the baby's father. David and Winter had been married for only six months. She was four months pregnant when David was killed. She spent the remainder of her pregnancy quietly, calmly, with as much serenity as she could create at High Hope. She oversaw the construction of the new offices she and David were to occupy. When construction was finished, she just let them sit until she had made a decision about them. She decided to call the baby Earle for a couple of reasons. Every time she uttered or heard the name "David," a streak of pain shot through her. And, like her grandmother, who insisted on calling her own husband by his middle name because she thought it more melodic, Winter thought Earle Thorpe was, if not particularly melodic, short and sweet. She knew that he, too, would be telling folks that there was an *e* at the end of his *Earl,* as his father had, making it easier to remember.

There could hardly be a moment of sadness during the succeeding four months as Roy, Ellen, and Winter raised Earle. They oohed and aahed over every little part of his development—the first time he smiled, the first time he uttered sounds in response to their attention to him. Winter kept him in a bassinette with her in the master bedroom downstairs while redecorating of the two bedrooms upstairs was taking place. Winter would move into one and Earle into the other so that she would be closer to him. Making a nursery out of one of the bedrooms was the highlight of all their lives. Roy painted and put up wallpaper. Ellen and Winter shopped for furniture and decorations. It was a beautiful nursery, and Winter couldn't wait for it to be finished. They could have had all of that prepared before Earle's birth, but Winter opted to wait so that she could live in quiet and peace for as long as she could before the baby's birth. She had worried about what effect the trauma she had experienced would have on the baby. Now, there was a flurry of activity.

Once in a while, as she passed the desk drawer that contained Lila's mysterious letter, she gave it an instant of thought, but only an instant. She would let nothing distract her from the advent of the birth of her son, her need to be quiet and at rest, and the joy of finally holding Earle in her arms. It wasn't long, however, until she gave the contents of that drawer more than an instant of thought.

Part Two

Chapter Eleven

It was in all the news reports, even the national news. A little two-year-old boy had accidentally fallen into a river that had begun to thaw from the winter freeze. His father tried desperately to get to him and pull him to shore, but the current caught the little boy and carried him downriver. His parents, joined by family, neighbors, firemen, police, and EMTs, frantically searched along the shore until finally they found him, caught on a piece of driftwood. By the time he was rescued and taken to the hospital, almost two hours had passed. Miraculously, he was warmed, reanimated, and suffered no ill effects from the event. This story, of course, caught the attention of the medical community, particularly that of Susan Wei.

Susan Wei was Lila's lifelong friend. They had been college roommates and sorority sisters. Susan was brilliant, probably genius level. While Lila was studying interior design, Susan raced through two degrees in medicine and biology. If it had not been for Lila, Susan would have had no social life at all. All she wanted to do was study, study, study. Lila would complain that they never had fun together, never went on double dates or to parties, except for a few sorority gatherings. Susan said that she was fascinated by what she was learning and couldn't wait to learn more. Finally, Lila prevailed, and Susan began to join her at social affairs, resulting in Susan meeting, falling in love with, and becoming engaged to another Asian student. Tragically, shortly after they had become engaged, Susan's fiancé was in a horrible swimming accident. He died, and Susan never had a man in her life again. She told Lila that she felt completely fulfilled with her studies and, later, her career.

After college, their paths went in different directions. Lila made quite a name for herself as an interior designer in Charlotte, where she met and married John Lassiter. Meanwhile, Susan determined that the clinical practice of medicine was not her cup of tea. Rather, she pursued a career in medical research, which had been her father's and grandfather's field in China. She concentrated on reanimation, which held a particular fascination for her. She dabbled in the subject of cryogenics, where people who had died would be frozen in the hope that a cure could be found for whatever had killed them, then thawed and brought back to life so that the appropriate cure or procedure could be applied. She quickly lost interest in that subject when it was determined that there were too many obstacles to the thawing-out process. Ice crystals damaged cell membranes, making them unable to function, thus making the organs and tissues they composed unable to function as well. It was reanimation after having died that grabbed Susan's interest. Ultimately, her focus turned from reanimating the deceased to the aging process that led inexorably to old age and death, even for people who had not suffered from any dread disease. With Lila's financial help, she developed two hundred acres, a farmhouse, a cabin, and other outbuildings into a research clinic in Zebron, a small rural suburb of Raleigh, North Carolina. She chose this location because of Duke University and its world-renowned medical and research center, and to be closer to her dear friend Lila in Bliss. She hired a staff of researchers, who delved into various aspects of the aging process on a molecular level, with the intent of finding ways to interfere with the process. They had made progress in this direction, thanks to their efforts and Lila's money.

Susan was to be the featured speaker at an Aging Symposium at the University of California, Los Angeles. She talked Lila into joining her to make a little vacation out of the trip. They hadn't been able to spend much time together during the past year. Even though she and Lila were both eighty-four, they were still quite active and busy. On the second night of their visit, they were enjoying dinner at one of the best steak houses in Los Angeles when Lila suddenly felt ill and then fell over—she'd had a heart attack.

Susan flew into action. She had six minutes to get blood flowing to Lila's brain, avoiding anoxia, or the death of brain cells. First, she assigned a fellow diner to start CPR, another to call 911 for an ambulance. In the ambulance, the EMTs were successful in shocking Lila's heart back into a somewhat regular beat, and oxygen was administered. Susan immediately directed that Lila's head be packed in napkins with ice from the kitchen, to ward against damage to her brain from the lack of blood supply. UCLA Medical Center was one of the few facilities equipped to perform a procedure that takes deoxygenated blood from a vein in the groin via a catheter, circulates the blood outside the body by means of a pump and a tube that passes through an oxygenator, then returns the newly oxygenated blood to the body through another catheter, into an artery in the groin and on to the heart that had been shocked into activity. This procedure served the function of the heart to reduce stress on the heart.

Once that was accomplished, she called John to give him the news and tell him that she was bringing Lila to Zebron. With her reputation preceding her, she had no difficulty getting the hospital to cooperate with whatever she wanted. Next, she arranged for a private jet to transport both of them and the borrowed oxygenator and other equipment to Duke University Hospital in Raleigh, where Susan could be in charge of Lila's care. Duke was another facility that could provide the oxygenation procedure and the specially designed pump. The plan was to allow Lila's head and brain to return slowly to normal temperature to avoid damage to the brain from lack of oxygen, in the hope that, just as for the little boy who had fallen into the freezing river, there would be no damage to her brain or other organs during her trip from California to Raleigh. The little boy was without oxygenated blood to his organs for two hours. The borrowed jet was sent back to California to return the equipment used to keep oxygenated blood flowing in Lila. Once stabilized, Susan's attention would turn to the imaging and tests that would determine what kind of heart attack Lila had experienced and to making plans for what to do about it. There were several options, depending on test results and how much heart muscle had been damaged.

It was determined that one of the four major coronary arteries had become completely blocked and that Lila's body had already produced collateral arteries to go around or bypass the blockage. One of these collateral arteries had become blocked, preventing either artery to allow blood to flow. Susan prevailed upon

the best coronary surgeon at Duke to operate immediately. He was able to clear both blockages, however,
the other three main coronary arteries were moder-
ately occluded, and Lila's heart muscle had been badly
damaged. Lila awoke from the anesthetic and was
somewhat alert with no obvious brain damage because
of the reduced demand for blood to her brain by having
been cooled with the ice pack, but the temporary
oxygenated blood transfer procedure was left intact
so as to continue to reduce stress to her heart, since
a good deal of her heart muscle had been damaged
by the attack. Then, Susan needed to let Lila's family
know what had occurred. It had been thirty-six hours
since the attack.

Chapter Twelve

As soon as Lila had become stable in Raleigh, Susan called her son John in Charlotte. She explained what had happened and asked him if he could come to Raleigh to discuss the matter with her. He agreed, explained to Grace, and headed that way immediately.

What he found at the Lassiter Medical Research Center was sobering, to say the least. Lila was in a hospital bed in the living room of the cabin Susan used as her residence. A nurse sat at a small desk nearby, monitoring various machines to which Lila had been connected. The nurse was asked to give Susan and John some privacy, so she left the room. While flying to Raleigh, Susan had made arrangements for everything that would be needed for Lila at the Center; Lila was being hydrated, her blood was being oxygenated, she was being minimally nourished, and she was receiving medications to keep her blood pressure within an acceptable range, but she was breathing on her own with the help of oxygen. Susan had put her into a chemically induced coma for the transfer to Raleigh. She needed to discuss with John the options going forward and whatever legal accommodations needed to be established, depending on the choice made as to the disposition of Lila's care.

John spent a few minutes with his mother, holding her hand and wiping his tears away. His first words to Susan were to ask if she was going to live, and if so, in what condition.

"John," Susan said, "she can be kept alive with a lot of medical help, but with her heart as damaged as it has been, that probably won't be a long-term solution. John, she needs a new heart."

"A new heart? As in a transplant?"

"That's probably not the best option at first, given the demand for transplantable hearts that her body would not reject. It's taking many months and sometimes years for an appropriate heart with a good match to be found. And, at eighty-four years old, she would be on the very bottom of the list."

"I don't understand. What other option for a new heart is there?"

"First, there is a temporary fix of a couple of kinds. An artificial mechanical heart has been developed that can be implanted in a patient's chest with electrodes leading from it through a portal in her skin to a box of batteries, which she would keep with her at all times, and the batteries would need to be kept charged. This would be temporary until a transferable heart could be found."

John stood quietly trying to process what Susan had told him.

"But, Susan, you have said that at eighty-four, she probably would not be eligible for a transplant. What would be the point of this 'mechanical heart'?"

Susan spoke again. "John, there is another option other than waiting for a human heart that could be successfully transplanted."

"What do you mean? Some kind of heart other than human?"

"No, no, John. It would be a human heart, in fact her own heart that, while she was connected to the artificial heart, was being reproduced and repaired."

"I don't understand what you are telling me."

"Come with me and I'll show you something that will better explain it."

Susan took John into the clinic and down a long hallway, passing several closed doors, until they came to the next to last door, with a sign that said "3D Bioprinting." Susan unlocked and opened the door and ushered John inside. The room was filled with many kinds of machines and equipment, all of which seemed to be connected to a glass box with the dimensions of a medium-sized aquarium. Inside the box was what appeared to John to be a lump of tissue. As he came closer, he saw something like a needle going back and forth across the lump. Susan explained to him what he was seeing.

"That tissue you see is being 3D bioprinted to ultimately become a kidney. An MRI of the patient's kidney was taken, then stem cells are taken from the patient and used to build a new kidney by copying the MRI image and fixing whatever was wrong with the kidney that caused it to stop functioning correctly. What you see that needle doing is releasing kidney cells. There is no chance of rejection, because it is made from the patient's own cells. This process has been used a number of times for copies of organs, skin, bones, lungs. Bioprinting the heart is more difficult because of the need to copy vasculature and nerves—the first success of this procedure was established just last month in China. Research is being done all over the world in countries that are not as burdened by regulations as the US. And a lot of work is being done behind closed doors with no oversight at all. When a procedure has been perfected and proven, it is sold to a legitimate research facility, usually at a university. They will then confirm findings, publish all the studies, write the peer-reviewed articles, and so forth. With the recent success of heart 3D bioprinting, I'd like to start the process for your mom to have her heart copied so as to replace her damaged heart."

John could only stand with eyes opened wide, trying to take in what Susan was telling him. It seemed foreign and far-fetched, yet there he was, watching a kidney being copied, using the patient's own kidney cells, from a kidney that had begun to malfunction. Being a lawyer, when he could finally speak, his questions were, "Are you talking about legally or illegally? What permits are required? Obviously, she is not able to give her permission. Are you asking me, as her next of kin, to authorize this? What are the chances that there will be complications and she will die anyway? What am I to tell Winter and others about this?"

Susan replied, "In answer to your first question, yes, if you want to stay on the legal side of things, your permission would be required. We would make application to the institute in China that has just successfully 3D bioprinted and implanted a heart. Remember that I have many connections in China, and this first step could be completed quickly. As to the success of this procedure for Lila, yes, there could be complications resulting in her death. We don't know what the long-term results will be from this first successful procedure. In the short term, everything looks perfect. This, as I have said, has only been done once. What and how much should be explained to Winter, Grace, and others would be entirely up to you. As I see it, your choices are to explain it all as

I have explained it to you, or you could let everyone believe that she has had a heart attack from which she did not recover and explain that she has donated her body to medical research, then have a memorial service. Thereafter, should there be complications that render the procedure unsuccessful, they will have already dealt with her death. If, on the other hand, it is successful and your mom has been returned to an apparently long-term healthy life, I should think the decision as to making this known to Winter and everyone involved should be Lila's. It would be an unusually difficult decision, taking into account all aspects of the impact of her having remained alive, but if anyone could handle this with wisdom and compassion, it would be Lila."

John just stood silently, looking at Susan, then the 3D bioprinting machine, then back at Susan. It was all more than he could comprehend. Making a decision whether to authorize this for his mother was not possible without a little time to weigh and consider everything. This he conveyed to Susan.

"Susan, you must know how hard this is for me. I had no idea that medical scientific achievements had come this far. I don't think anybody outside the medical community is aware of this. At first blush, I think what you are asking of me is to give my permission for Mother to be, well, sort of a guinea pig. I can't give you an answer now, Susan. I need a little time to sort this out—think it through—during the few hours it will take me to drive back to Charlotte. I know I'll have to tell the family something when I get back. I just don't know what right now. I'll let you know what I've decided later today."

"Of course, John," Susan replied. "I know full well what a difficult decision this is. Think about it. Call me if you have any questions. Otherwise, I'll wait to hear from you this evening. John, I can't help you with this. I can't in good conscience try to influence you one way or the other. You know how much I love Lila and have since we were college kids. Honestly, I wouldn't want to have to make this decision that I have thrust upon you."

With that, Susan gave John a perfunctory hug, and John turned to leave. He glanced at the signs on the other doors in the hallway as he walked through: "Cell Senescence," "Bio-chemical," "Genomics"—all very strange to him.

As he walked toward his car, it began to rain. How appropriate, he thought, that the weather should reflect his feelings about what he had just experienced. He felt confused, frightened, anxious, and almost dizzy in his effort to think clearly. Before he got up on the road to Charlotte, he stopped at a café for a cup of coffee and to try to calm down.

As he sat with closed eyes, breathing deeply, the sound of a woman and a girl sitting at a nearby table drew his attention. The girl looked to be about fifteen or sixteen, the age of his Winter. Winter. What can I tell Winter at this tender age, knowing how deeply she loves her grandmother?

Finally, he got on his way, totally distracted from his driving with trying to consider all aspects of the decision with which he was grappling. What to do? What to do? By the time he got back to Charlotte, he had made his decision and called Susan immediately.

Chapter Thirteen

John Lassiter was, like his father had been, a very conservative man, one who had trouble with the technological innovations of the day. There was an instant resistance to the medical advances Susan had described to him. To his way of thinking, it was unnatural. Life consisted of being born, maturing, growing old, and dying. That's the way it had always been, the way it always should be. He brought this point of view to his deliberations about his mother's future.

Additionally, he thought about whether what Susan proposed for a new heart for his mother was a crap shoot. Would it be successful, or would it not? If it were not, then Lila's loved ones would have to go through the pain of Lila's death at that time, rather than right now, and only after having had to cope with what was happening to Lila and the ultimately dashed hope that she would survive. Susan had explained to him that if all the medical equipment being used to keep Lila alive were taken away, she would in all probability die very shortly thereafter.

All things considered, John decided to tell Susan that he would not be giving permission for the procedure she proposed and, furthermore, that he would direct all the medical equipment being used to keep her alive to be disconnected. As far he was concerned, and as he would tell the family, Lila had a massive heart attack and died in California, where her body was donated to the University of California for scientific research, in accordance with her wishes. A memorial service would be held, and that would be the end of it—as was natural, as it should be. No being used as a guinea pig, no crap shoot, no exotic means of allowing her to live longer than, apparently, the good Lord intended. This was the position he took when he called Susan after returning to Charlotte.

Susan, actually, was not surprised. Over the years, Lila had made her aware of Gordon's temperament and that, either by nature or nurture or both, John had inherited the same way of thinking. For the Lassiter men, if one couldn't see, hear, or touch something, it didn't exist, like radio waves, totally incomprehensible to both of them, much less the technological advances being introduced to their lives almost daily.

Until Lila had understood Gordon's way of thinking, there had been some strife between them, as Lila, having an innovative, imaginative, creative, curious mind, challenged Gordon to use critical thinking in learning about something new. He wasn't interested in learning about new things. The way things always had been suited him just fine. Change was anathema to him. When she accepted that Gordon's way of thinking was just as valid and valuable as her own, she came to depend upon his point of view in various matters. He was a very detail-oriented person, making him a wonderful architect where details could make or break a project. It was Lila's conceptualistic mind that made her a successful interior designer. Gordon called it "Lila being in a trance" when she would sit in a room for a long time, taking in what the room looked like and then what she was to make it look like.

In anticipation of the nature of his decision, Susan had already begun the process of awakening Lila from the chemically induced coma in which she had put her. Lila needed to be in her right mind to decide for herself what was to be done, after everything had been explained to her. John, nor anyone else, would ever need to know unless Lila wanted them to. In accordance with John's dictate, all the equipment to which Lila was connected would be disconnected. Nothing was said in his order, however, about a mechanical heart pump, an LVAD. Susan immediately went about making arrangements for that to happen, beginning with taking her to Duke to have the pump attached to her heart, with an electrode leading from the pump, via a portal through her skin in her abdomen, to a box full of batteries to keep the heart pumping with electricity provided by the batteries. It was a temporary solution until a heart transplant could be achieved. Meanwhile, the box of batteries needed to be kept with her at all times, and the batteries needed to be kept charged.

Lila's first full conscious moments were in the living room of the cabin with Susan sitting beside her. The MRI had been accomplished and the "heart in a box" installed. Susan told Lila what had happened and where she was. Beyond that, Susan told her that there was much they needed to discuss, but that could wait until the next day, after she was fully aware and could sit up and eat a little something. She needed to be able to hear and understand everything Susan was to explain to her. Lila spent the night sleeping off and on, wondering and thinking about the conversation Susan wanted to have with her the next day.

Chapter Fourteen

It was a beautiful autumn day, the temperature having begun to cool, perfect for sitting in the sun with a cool breeze on the patio in front of the research center. Lila had had a good night in Susan's cabin, despite being awakened by her nurse for taking vitals and administering medications, then becoming immersed in her thoughts until she could get back to sleep. Susan and Lila's nurse took her off the monitor and saline drip, got her in a wheelchair, and rolled her, along with the oxygenation pump, oxygen tank, and "heart in a box," out onto the patio. After both women were settled, Lila began questioning Susan.

"Okay, Susan, what's going on? I understand that I had a heart attack in California and that in some miraculous way that only you could pull off, you got me here within hours, got my blocked arteries unblocked, got this machine hooked up to me, and got me here to the Center. Have you been in touch with John?"

"Yes, Lila, John was here with you yesterday, but I had you in a light coma so we could get you here from Duke comfortably and through surgery. You weren't awake for his visit."

"Oka-a-ay. So now what? How long will I need this machine?"

"Lila, I need you to listen to me carefully. Your heart muscle has been badly damaged. That's why you are hooked up to this pump, to help your weakened heart keep your blood oxygenated and flowing. Without this pump, life expectancy for you is a very short time, but we can't keep you on this pump forever. You need a new heart."

"A new heart? How am I going to get a new heart at eighty-four?"

"That won't happen in the traditional way of putting you on a transplant list and waiting for an appropriate donor. But there are other alternatives."

"Yeah, like what?"

"Lila, what I am about to explain to you is highly technical, so I'm going to oversimplify it and talk in terms of the bottom line for your understanding. As the primary benefactor of the Lassiter Research Center, I've been keeping you apprised of our work here . . . mostly. There are things we've been doing, here and in China, that are cutting edge and not quite ready for prime time."

"Not ready for prime time? I'm not sure I understand. Have you been doing something illegal?"

"Not illegal in China. I've told you about the fantastic work that has been done with 3D bioprinting. The first medical applications were for reproducing skin and used mostly by the Veterans Administration for their burn victims. Burns are the most common injury for our military personnel. With this procedure having been perfected, researchers went on to other applications of 3D bioprinting, moving on to reproducing organs. We have 3D bioprinters here, and at this moment, a kidney is being reproduced."

"You're right. This is all way over my head, and I appreciate your trying to make it simple and understandable, though I'm not sure I do understand it. What does all this have to do with my condition and health?"

"Progress has been moving right along with the wonders of this technology. Researchers hit a stumbling block with organs that had more vasculature and nerve pathways involved, the main one being the heart. Just last month, however, a research center in China has been successful in 3D bioprinting a human heart and implanting it in the patient."

"Good Lord! What's going to be next? Bioprinting a whole human being?"

"That's being done in certain highly secret places by cloning humans."

"Secret places?"

"Yes. You know that in the United States, this is forbidden. Early on, scientists were not allowed to let embryonic cells multiply beyond fourteen times. Left alone to continue to replicate, we're talking about letting a baby develop. Now, several other countries will adopt the same rules in the future. But there are places on the planet now where no such restrictions exist, and research scientists refuse to be stopped from pursuing the possibilities of science."

"So, have humans actually been cloned?"

"Yes. In two cases. But you understand this is not information that can ever be revealed."

"Of course. And, actually, I'm not surprised. I've been close enough to your work to realize the potential for developments that could only be imagined. But again, what does all of this have to do with me? Are you planning to have me cloned?"

When the laughter subsided, Susan replied, "Heavens, no! The world could stand only one of you! But, who knows. Meanwhile, the plan is, with your approval, to 3D bioprint your heart."

"My approval? What are the risks?"

"This has been achieved only once, just last month. So far, so good, but obviously we can't know about the long term, or what complications might arise that might ultimately make the procedure unsuccessful."

"Why me, Susan—at eighty-four? I might not want to live much longer and get senile and decrepit. You know, we've had this discussion, both of us being the same age."

Susan picked up Lila's arm and put it next to hers. Lila's skin had become typically thin and crepey. Susan's skin was that of a woman decades younger. Lila looked at their arms, then at Susan.

"I have always been jealous of your Asian skin. Your face looks like a fresh spanked baby's butt, and mine is wrinkled and sagging. It's not fair!"

"Lila, it's true that the texture of skin of people of Asian descent is different from that of others, but that's not the only reason my skin looks like it does."

"Well, what do you mean? What other reasons?"

"Lila, we'll get into that at another time. Right now, we need to be deciding what to do about your weakened heart."

"Did you explain all of this to John?"

"Yes, I did. And I explained that until you were in your right mind, after the effect of anesthesia and the light coma I had put you in was all over, I would need his legal permission to begin this process."

"And?"

"Lila, he declined. First, I think all of the technology scared him to death. You know how Gordon thought. Gordon would have thought this was all too unnatural.

John thinks the same way. He has told the family that you had a heart attack and died in California and that you had previously arranged for your body to be donated for scientific medical research. There is to be a memorial service for you in the next day or two. He was most concerned about Winter and the prospect of your going through with this, only to have you die from complications in the future, after her being so thrilled with your having been revived to live longer. He felt it would be too cruel to give her false hope. It was his opinion that it would be best for Winter to believe you were gone now, allowing her to cope with your death and move on with her life, rather than be in a constant state of worry that some complication would take you away from her. You were going to die at some point in time, and it would impact Winter traumatically whenever that occurred. He further directed me to take you off of all the equipment that was keeping you alive at that time. Bioprinting will take longer than for some other applications, because it is done in three separate stages."

"Whoa. Whoa. Wait. Let me make sure I understand. Everybody has already been told that I am dead and there's to be a memorial service?"

"Exactly. John felt that putting you through the bioprinting and implantation of a new heart at this point in the science would be tantamount to making a guinea pig out of you, and he couldn't agree to that. He said he thought it best to let nature take its course, which would mean that without intervention, you wouldn't be here for probably more than a month or so with the condition your heart muscle is in. So, Lila, right or wrong, it was my opinion that you should have the opportunity to make this decision for yourself."

After a long silence, Lila reached for Susan's hand. "Thank you," she said. "Thank you for knowing me well enough and loving me that much to let me decide for myself. You know I'm going to have to think long and hard about this."

"Of course, I defied John's instructions to disconnect you from everything and had the LVAD installed."

"Okay, good. I'm tired now, Susan. Can I go back to the cabin?"

Susan texted the nurse, and together, they got Lila back in the hospital bed in Susan's cabin and made comfortable. After they left, Lila lay looking at the ceiling, her mind racing with the information she had just heard. What rose to the top of her thoughts was that everyone she loved thought she was dead. Tears began to flow, and a monitor began to beep. The nurse hurried in and injected a sedative to calm her down. Lila drifted off to sleep, reminding herself that one cannot think clearly and feel strongly at the same time. She was too emotional to do any constructive thinking about whether she wanted to live or be allowed to die. Like Scarlett O'Hara in *Gone with the Wind*, her last thought was, "I'll think about that tomorrow."

Chapter Fifteen

Tomorrow arrived, as all tomorrows do. The only thing on Lila's to-do list was to think about the decision Susan had tasked her to make. The first thing that came to her mind was Winter. In her imagination, she saw Winter at the memorial service, inconsolably crying, unable to receive any words of comfort from anyone. Lila had to quickly turn the page on that vision, lest she should have to be sedated again. On her eightieth birthday, she had tried to discuss with Winter what would surely be her death in the not-too-distant future. However, Winter would have none of it. "Oh, Grandmother," she'd said, "we all know you're going to live to be one hundred."

Lila concluded that John had been right. Should Winter be made aware of the heart replacement procedure, with its unknown long-term success, Winter's life would be dominated by fear that failure would occur and her grandmother would die. Not knowing how long that might be, Lila decided that it would be unfair to put Winter through that kind of agony, especially now that she had been told that her grandmother had already died and was dealing with the finality and sorrow of that knowledge. So that part of the decision was made. If Lila decided to proceed with the heart replacement, Winter would not be told until there was sufficient evidence that the procedure had indeed been successful. But how many years would it take to arrive at that conclusion? And how big a shock would that be to Winter whenever she was told that her grandmother was alive? What impact on her life?

Before considering answers to those questions, Lila next turned to thinking about herself and how much longer she might want to live. As she had reminded Susan, they had already had the conversation on that subject. Lila's life had always been one of activity and competence. Even past the age of eighty, she had continued to do selective interior design projects very successfully. Then, Lila remembered what Susan had remarked about the difference between them in the appearance of their same-aged bodies, and the comment that this was a subject that was to be discussed at a later time. Susan, too, had continued to live a very active and productive life in her eighties. Lila decided that before she could decide how much longer she wanted to live, the time for her to discuss later was now. She called Susan to come talk to her.

Susan came to the cabin, and after they had settled down with a cup of tea, Lila broached the subject.

"Susan, I want to talk about what you referred to previously as the reason you appear to be so much younger than I. What were you talking about?"

"Lila, again I am going to try to make an extremely complex subject understandable to you through over-simplification. You know that my field of research and no small degree of expertise have been in the area of anti-aging. Through research, we have discovered several things that cause cell aging and have found, on a molecular level, chemical ways to interfere with that process. I'll give you one example, but there have been several, and there are many more to discover. At the end of each DNA strand are segments that could not be identified to code for anything. They're call telomeres. However, each time a cell divides, a telomere in the nucleus of a chromosome is lost, dropped off."

"Whoa, Susan. If that is your idea of making technical things oversimplified for layman's understanding, that's a piss poor attempt. I can't grasp even the essence of what you are trying to tell me. Just get to the bottom line."

"Okay, bottom line. We have created and devised a protocol for stopping the aging process and even to some extent reversing it. I've been the clinical testing guinea pig, along with some other volunteers in China. That's why I look so much younger than you."

"Well, I'll be damned! You did it! You actually did it! You've spent your whole life trying to achieve this, and you finally did."

"Yes, Lila. It would appear so. And this is what is to be included in the course of action to keep you living for many more years with vitality and vigor."

"In other words, my heart can be replaced with a brand-new one, and I can start the program that is to make me stop aging, even become a little younger?"

"Exactly, Lila. Exactly."

"Wow. That's a lot to take in."

"Lila, if you only knew what I know about the future of anti-aging pursuits, you'd be astonished."

"Well, you've given me a lot more to think about. As if I needed more! I'll decide before long. You'll be the first to know whether I have decided to live or die. And, Susan, again, I'm grateful to you for allowing that decision to be made by me. You know what a control freak I am. To know that I am in control of my life or death is very satisfying."

"Yes, of course, I have known that about you. I hope you won't take too long to decide."

"The primary thing I am trying to get my head around is if everything goes as hoped for, my heart is bioprinted, fixed, and implanted, and we wait to see if it is actually going to be successful, how long should we wait to make that determination before I let Winter know I'm alive?"

"Lila, I think there are too many unknowns to try to determine that at this time. I suggest we take it one day at a time."

Lila and Susan sat quietly for the next few minutes, with Lila deep in thought. Finally, she said, "Susan, in addition to my being a control freak, you have also known me to be a risk taker and to love an adventure. What the hell? Let's do it! As you say, we'll take it one day at a time. Besides, I have donated my body to medical research, haven't I?"

And so began the greatest adventure Lila could ever have imagined, that day having been the first day of one day at a time. Susan smiled broadly, gave Lila a hug and a kiss on her forehead, then hustled off to begin putting the adventure into motion.

Chapter Sixteen

As a first step, Susan was having the MRI of Lila's heart 3D bioprinted in silicone so that surgeons could determine how to repair the reduced blood supply to the heart muscle that had damaged it, causing the heart attack. Blood vessels and nerves also needed to be 3D bioprinted. They could then practice on the silicone heart doing what needed to be done surgically to the new heart 3D bioprinted from Lila's heart stem cells. Embryonic stem cells, as those taken from umbilical cord blood, could be used to form any part of the human anatomy. Adult stem cells, however, are organ-specific. Stem cells for heart muscle, blood vessels, and nerves would need to be taken from Lila's body.

This work was being done in China at the clinic created by Susan's grandfather and then run by her father. The surgery to implant Lila's new heart would be done there as well, but not by her father. A world-renowned surgeon was affiliated with the clinic and performed any surgeries needed in their research pursuits. Therefore, while Winter was studying for six years to get all of her degrees, Lila was also studying—the Chinese language. This was a godsend for Lila, as she was constantly grappling with the matter of Winter not knowing that she was alive and waiting for Winter to respond to the letter she was to be given upon her parents' deaths.

As time passed, Lila subscribed to the local Watauga County newspaper. It was from that source she would learn of Winter's graduations—from high school, from college with a BA, with her master's degree and doctorate—the establishment of her psychology practice in Charlotte; the deaths of her parents; her marriage; then the death of her new husband. The Lassiter name had become quite prominent in the county, making anything having to do with any of the Lassiters newsworthy. Just as she had been thinking perhaps she could be sure that she could continue living healthily for even more years, and the time had come to let Winter know she was alive, one of these traumas occurred, and she knew she could not add additional trauma to Winter's life, which receiving this news would be. So time passed, one year following the other, until, suddenly it seemed, seventeen years had passed.

There was an additional reason Susan needed Lila to go to China.

Inner Mongolia is one of the very few places in the world where the best astragalus herb can be grown. Astragalus, a member of the pea family, is primarily used to stimulate the immune system. It is therefore highly sought. Astragalus root was an important part of Susan's anti-aging protocol, so important to Susan, as well as to many others who seek it, that she purchased property in Inner Mongolia to grow and sell it. Being Chinese, Susan often visited her family in China, and when she did, she included a brief visit to the astragalus fields to meet with her grower and her marketing manager and to visit the facility where, after being harvested during a brief window of time at the end of fall, but before the winter storms arrived, the root was milled and prepared for sale.

Inner Mongolia is a long, crescent-shaped strip of Eastern Mongolia, bordered on the south and east by China, on the west by Mongolia, and on the north by Russia. Much like, when cultivating and growing grapes for wine, specific regions are most successfully productive, for astragalus, the grasslands at the foot of the Blue Mountains in Ordos, Inner Mongolia, had been found to be the very best for its production

Inner Mongolian grasslands had been deteriorating for many years due to wind blowing desert sands into the grasslands and because of overgrazing by sheep and yaks. The ecological situation had become so dire that attractive offers had been made by the Chinese government for farmers to grow crops that were sustainable in the grassland areas to stabilize and recover them. When this information came to Susan, after consultation with the appropriate entities, she purchased several acres of land on which to cultivate astragalus, which grew well in that location.

Susan's goal was to find land in the United States similar to that in Inner Mongolia, on which astragalus could be successfully grown. Her research on the subject revealed that among the best places in the US were areas at the foot of the Appalachian Mountains. High Hope's acreage would be perfect for that use.

Susan needed to spend some time in Hohhot, the capital of Inner Mongolia, to learn all she could from her farm supervisor about all the details of how to grow astragalus successfully. But this was time Susan did not have. So she prevailed upon Lila to spend that time for this purpose in Hohhot and at the Lassiter Medicinal Herb Company to acquire the needed information and knowledge. This, too, was welcomed by Lila, to keep her from going crazy worrying about Winter, missing her and High Hope terribly, worrying about how successful all Susan's plans for her health might be, and prognosticating about how much longer she might live.

One day at a time ultimately stretched into seventeen years of surgery, recovery, monitoring for complications, and continually getting stronger, healthier, mentally sharper, and, yes, even looking younger. Seventeen years of guilt for not having been with Winter through all her tragedies. Seventeen years of trying to protect Winter from more trauma while she was getting her education, going through the various tragedies, and then pregnancy. And getting busier and busier in Inner Mongolia with astragalus concerns, as well as researching the best soil and climate conditions for growing many other medicinal herbs, such as *Angelica dahurica,* a flowering perennial whose root is used to relieve pain and inflammation; *Aster tataricus,* a relative of garden asters said to have antibacterial properties; *Mentha haplocalyx,* a mint used for stomach ailments; and *Salvia miltiorrhiza,* a type of sage whose roots are used for treatment of cardiovascular diseases, as well as many other herbs. Lila and Susan were to become "pharma-farmers" in the US.

Chapter Seventeen

It has been said that if man can imagine it, he can create it. There is ample evidence of the truth of this throughout history, beginning with the invention of the wheel. The cloning of Dolly the sheep opened a Pandora's box for the use of embryonic stem cells. Furious debates ensued as to the use of cloning human stem cells. Initially, twelve countries agreed to allow human stem cell division in a petri dish to occur up to fourteen times for therapeutic purposes. China was not one of those countries until, ultimately, when a total of thirty countries were in agreement on the issue. By that time, however, scientists in China had exercised their choice of allowing cell division to continue far beyond fourteen times, resulting in the surreptitious cloning of a human being.

Dolly the sheep was not the first cloned animal as claimed. Animals had been cloned years before Dolly—frogs and other critters. Then, subsequently, cloning had been accomplished with several other mammals, and finally, Macaque monkeys had been cloned, with the closest DNA to that of a human. Wealthy people were paying as much as fifty thousand dollars to have their beloved pets cloned. These clonings were done in the same way Dolly was cloned. An egg was taken from a female sheep; its nucleus, containing the DNA of that sheep, was removed and replaced with the nucleus of a stem cell. After several cell divisions, it was placed in the womb of another sheep to gestate, just like in vitro fertilization was performed, except the cells placed in the female sheep for gestation were the exact duplicate of the donor sheep, not the combination of DNA from a female and a male.

A scientist in Italy announced to the world that a successful cloning of a female baby had been accomplished, using this method with a surrogate mother. All appeared to be perfectly normal with the baby as they monitored her development after birth, and they named her Eve. Neither this cloned baby nor its mother has ever been seen, nor has any kind of proof of this event been satisfactorily provided. However, a lawsuit was filed against the company making this claim for the purpose of designating a temporary guardian for Eve for fear she would be used as a "lab rat." Since then, many more claims have been made of cloned babies having been born, in various countries, regardless of the fact that it was illegal in thirty countries. The company that purportedly performed the cloning stated that it had received numerous requests for the procedure, particularly from the entertainment industry in California, which they steadfastly had refused. They were open, they said, to the cloning of children for acceptable reasons. Since it continues to be illegal, everything about this endeavor was done secretly and well protected from the authorities, until the decision was made to announce the cloning of Eve.

Concurrently, in other research labs, artificial wombs were being developed. The original purpose for this pursuit was to allow very premature babies to be placed into what had been dubbed "biobags" to complete gestation, giving them a greater chance for continued development into viable babies. The first of these experiments was performed on three lambs, delivered prematurely by cesarean section and placed into a biobag that had been equipped with everything needed for continued gestation, including a sort of umbilical cord through which blood and nutrients were delivered to the embryos, an enzymatic solution mimicking amniotic fluid, and a filtering process that eliminated waste products. Scientists watched with tremendous excitement to view the lambs in the clear plastic biobag as they developed, moving their legs, opening and closing their mouths.

It was only a matter of time before these two developments merged into the ability to clone a human by way of a few embryonic cell divisions placed into an artificial womb to develop, not during the last couple of months of normal gestation, but at the very beginning of the life of a human. Unknown to the world at large, Susan's father had accomplished this at his lab in China.

Part Three

Chapter Eighteen

It had been almost thirteen years since Lila's "death." Once again, on the last of many such occasions, Susan found Lila crying over her separation from Winter. Susan asked, "Why, Lila, don't you just reach out to her?"

"Susan, can you imagine what a shock this will be to her? What a trauma? How it would impact her life? She is just now starting her practice of psychology in Charlotte. How could I justify upsetting her life with that call to relieve me of my own sorrow and guilt? I know the time will come when Winter will be given the letter I wrote to her. By that time, I hope, she'll be a little older, a little more mature, a little more capable of dealing with the fact that I'm not dead."

"Okay, Lila. This is your choice. I just hate so much to see you in such distress. I wish there were something I could do for you." Susan decided then and there that there *was* something she could do that might help Lila.

In 1992, the first company was formed to save umbilical cord blood from delivered babies so that embryonic stem cells could be harvested from that blood. With embryonic stem cells, any part of the human body, or the entire body, could be cloned. These stem cells could be inserted into any organ of the body to reproduce and replace diseased parts of that organ, or they could be used to create an entire organ to replace a diseased one.

Winter was seven years old when the cord blood saving company was formed. Susan and her father, however, had become aware that "adult" stem cells could be transformed into embryonic cells. On a visit by Susan with Lila and Winter, for Winter's seventh birthday, Susan removed some skin cells from Winter and had them made into embryonic cells, lots of them, and frozen for future use should the need arise. Now, Susan thought maybe that need had arrived.

One day, when Susan and Lila were chatting over a glass of wine, Susan said, "Wouldn't it be wonderful if you could experience Winter's birth again and watch her grow up?"

Lila looked at Susan quizzically and said, "What an odd question. Of course, that would be fantastically awesome, but could never be. Why would you ask such a question, Susan?"

"Oh, I was just imagining things, as I often do. Silly of me, I suppose."

Susan immediately went to her father and explained

that she wanted to clone Winter, and why. The embryonic cells were thawed, with only three of them surviving the process. They were allowed to replicate in a petri dish over four weeks then were implanted into an artificial uterus that had become perfected in its function. Only one of the cells successfully attached itself to the artificially created uterine lining. After nine months, the cloned Winter was "delivered," thoroughly examined, and found to be normal and healthy.

When the baby was two months old, she was flown to Susan in North Carolina, where she was to be cared for in one of the administrative office rooms at Lassiter Medical Research Center until Susan had made the baby's presence known to Lila. Susan thought long and hard about how and when she would tell Lila that she could have Winter back as a newborn baby. She chose a beautiful day when she and Lila took their walk through the woods, as they often did. They had placed a bench along the route on which to sit, rest, and talk midway through their walk. This time, their talk would be earth shattering for Lila.

"Lila, do you remember last year when I asked you about how it would feel to have Winter back as a newborn baby, and you said it would be fantastically awesome?"

"Yes, I think I remember that. What are you getting at?"

"There's something specific and special we need to talk about today."

"Really. Pray tell, what?"

Susan began by reminding her of previous times when she had tried, in simple terms, to describe her work to Lila and let her view cells through the microscope. Then she went on to explain what had been done over the years with embryonic cells.

"Amazing," Lila said. Then Susan reminded her of the time that she had taken some skin cells from Winter when she was seven to have them transferred into embryonic cells and frozen. "Yes," Lila said, "I remember that."

"Lila, hold on to yourself now. I have something to tell you that will come as something of a shock. There's no better way to tell you other than just coming out with it. My father and I have used one of Winter's embryonic cells to create a clone of her. The baby is two months old now, and is at this moment in the administrative building. You can have your Winter back, in a way, without risking any terrible trauma you have feared so much for the original Winter."

Lila just sat and stared at Susan, trying to wrap her mind around what Susan had told her. Then, her lip started quivering, and a flood of tears began dripping off her chin. When she was finally able to speak, her first question was, "But Susan, who is to raise her? Even with your anti-aging protocol, I'm still eighty-two or -three instead of the ninety-eight I would have been by now. How long will I be able to care for and raise an infant?"

"There are options; depending upon circumstances at the time, that question will need to be answered. In the meantime, would you like to meet the baby?"

"Yes. You say she's in the administrative building?"

"Well, actually, I had Deborah follow us at a distance with instructions to bring her to us when I called." Deborah had been hired as the Lassiter Medical Research Center receptionist several years earlier.

With that, Susan took her phone out of her pocket, dialed, and said, "Okay, Deb. Bring the baby to us."

In just a minute or two, Deborah approached with the baby in her arms. Susan reached for the baby, and Deborah passed her over and left. Lila could clearly see the baby from that angle. Susan took the pacifier that had been used to keep the baby quiet out of her mouth. It took Lila's breath away to look at the same baby she had first seen twenty-eight years before. The same beautiful baby with wisps of auburn hair, dark brown eyes, and a rosebud mouth. All Lila could do was hold the baby's hand and cry and cry. At last, she said to Susan, "Thank you, Susan. Oh, thank you. I don't know what to feel except love of you for wanting to do this for me." At that point, Susan was crying, too. Then the baby started crying, and there the three of them sat on that bench in the woods, crying. After a few minutes, the pacifier was replaced in the baby's mouth, noses were blown, and tears were dried.

"Shall we head back?" Susan asked. "We've got a lot to do to accommodate this little angel. I know you'll want to take care of her, at least for a while."

"Yes," Lila replied, "but you'll need to carry her. I'm shaking too much to feel safe holding her." So off they went to begin a new chapter in Lila's life, a chapter she had no idea how to pursue. But, as Lila had done throughout her life, she was able to respond, then adapt, then make lemonade out of lemons.

Chapter Nineteen

"For a while" turned out to be four years. The first thing Susan did the day after Lila was shown the baby was to have a meeting with all Lassiter Medical Research Center personnel. She explained that a young female member of the Lassiter family had given birth to a baby whom she could not care for. There was no one else in the family to care for the baby girl, except for Lila. Furthermore, she explained that it was as yet unclear how long the baby would be there under Lila's care. During the ensuing four years, Winter's clone had the run of the laboratory from time to time. Everyone loved her, and it would not be unusual to find a researcher with the child sitting on a stool being instructed on how to look into a microscope, with an age-appropriate explanation as to what she was seeing.

A second cabin with bedrooms for Lila and the baby was built. Lila enjoyed the interior design of the new cabin. While Winter was learning how to be a mother to her newborn, David Earle, cloned Winter had begun being tutored at three years old, spending two hours five days per week with a tutor. By the time she was four years old, she could speak Mandarin Chinese as well as English. Sometimes she called Lila "Grandmother," sometimes "Zumu" (Zuhmuh). For Susan, sometimes she called her Auntie Sue, sometimes "Guma" (Goomay). Watching her grow and learn was the delight of Lila's life, and of Susan's. As was the case with the original Winter, Lila enjoyed her so much. They had lots of fun together. Not being exposed yet to other children in school, the question of having a mommy and a daddy had not come up. But it soon would. Lila and Susan had many conversations about the matter, but without arriving at an acceptable conclusion.

While Lila and Susan considered this issue frequently, Winter had become comfortable as a new mother. Earle was the joy of her life. There was no room in her heart or mind for thinking about the tragedies that had occurred in the past. She had, at last, come to that all-is-well place in her life, except for one thing.

One day, Winter sat down at her desk, and sitting right in the middle of it was Lila's letter. She wondered how it had gotten there and then reread it. Ellen took note of this in passing through the room and stopped to field the question she knew would be coming from Winter.

"Ellen, did you put Grandmother's letter on the desk?"

"Yes, sweetheart, I did."

"Why?"

"Winter, I have been so happy to see you finally content. When I saw you frequently stop by your desk, jerk open that drawer, then quickly shut it again, I became curious and found the letter. I knew that one day you would have to find out about Lila, so I just waited until that time came. I may be wrong, but in your present state of mind, I figured you were strong enough now to cope with whatever may be in store for you about it. I hope you'll consider making that call and get whatever comes of it behind us. What do you think?"

Winter sat staring at Ellen, thinking how grateful she was for her, and for her wisdom. She looked at Ellen, back at the letter she held in her hand, back and forth. After one last glance at Ellen, she picked up the phone and dialed the number written in the letter.

A receptionist answered the phone.

"Good afternoon, Lassiter Medical Research Center. This is Deborah. How can I help you?"

"Hello, Deborah, this is Winter Lassiter Thorpe, and—"

"Oh, Miss Lassiter! Dr. Wei has been expecting your call for a very long time. If you'll hold on for just a second, I'll connect you with her."

Winter sat with her mind whirling. Suddenly, Susan came on the line.

"Winter! I can't tell you how good it is to hear from you. Lila and I have been waiting for this call for . . . it's been almost seventeen years now. How are you?"

"Well, at the moment, Susan, I am confused and anxious. You say you and Grandmother have been waiting for my call. I can't believe I am speaking to you. By now you should be about—let me see—one hundred and one, but you sound just like you did at Grandmother's memorial service. How can this be?"

"There is so much that needs to be explained to you, Winter. Not only am I still alive, but your grandmother is, too. How soon can you come to Zebron?"

"Well, well, I guess tomorrow. You say Grandmother is there?"

"Yes, Winter, and I can't wait to tell her you are coming. She will be thrilled beyond words."

"Okay. I should be there around two tomorrow afternoon."

"See you then, Winter. Now let me go find your grandmother. Bye bye."

Winter hung up the phone and reached for Ellen. "You heard my end of the conversation." Ellen nodded.

"Susan said Grandmother was alive there in Zebron. I can't believe this. How can this be true? Why has she not let me know this for seventeen years? Seventeen years! She doesn't even know she has a great grandson."

"Well," Ellen said, "we'll soon find out what it's all about. Should be most interesting. Please tell Lila when you see her that Roy and I love her and can't wait to see her ourselves."

Meanwhile, Susan rushed off to find Lila. She found her in her cabin listening to a Chinese-language audio tape. She shut it off and looked at Susan, who seemed to be quite exhilarated. Susan sat down beside Lila and took her hand.

"Lila, what you have wanted for so long has happened."

"What has happened?"

"Lila, Winter called a few minutes ago and will be here tomorrow afternoon."

Lila's hands flew to her face, eyes opened wide. It took a couple of minutes for what Susan had told her to register. Then her mind began jumping from one thing to another. How would Winter react to seeing her, and seeing her so much younger than her years? How could she tell her that she had been cloned? And on and on, one unanswerable question after another. She barely slept at all that night.

The Lassiter Medical Research Center administrative building had once been a beautiful farmhouse with a circular drive. In the middle of the drive was a rose garden. As Winter drove up to the front door, she noticed a couple of people in the garden. It reminded her of how much her grandmother had loved her own rose garden. How could she have known that those people were her grandmother and her own clone?

As she opened the car door and started to crawl out, she realized that her knees were shaking, and so were her hands. She was feeling some combination of trepidation and joyful anticipation.

As Winter opened the door to the Center and stepped inside, Susan was already there waiting for her and approached her with arms opened wide. They hugged, and then Winter stepped back to get a good look at Susan. It was incredible, unbelievable—Susan looked no older than when she had last seen her.

"Come, Winter, let's go into my office. We have so much to talk about, and I know you have a million questions."

"Yes, I surely do. But, Susan, when can I see Grandmother?"

Susan turned to Deborah and asked her to find Lila. Once in the office, Susan began speaking.

"Winter, I think probably one of your first questions is how it is that I look so much younger than I actually am. You'll find that to be true for your grandmother, too. Winter, several years ago, I developed a chemical protocol that stopped the aging process and even reversed it to some degree. Your grandmother and I have been the first of the guinea pigs. It's in Phase 3 clinical trials now, then I'll be waiting for FDA approval and a patent for the process."

"My God, how fabulous. When can I become a guinea pig too?"

Before Susan could answer, the door flew open and a little girl burst in, running to Susan.

"Auntie Sue! Auntie Sue! Look what I've brought you."

The little girl thrust a rose toward Susan, and as Susan began to take it, the little girl pulled it away and, with all the seriousness she could muster, with her index finger stuck up in the air indicating caution, she said, "Auntie Sue, you have to be very, very careful. Roses have thorns on the stem, and if you stick yourself on one of them, it will hurt really, really bad. I know because I've been stuck. So be very careful, okay?"

Susan and Winter both smiled at this adorable child, then Susan said, "Thank you, yes, I'll be careful.

We have a visitor. Can you say hello?"

The little girl turned toward Winter and looked at her quizzically. Winter said, "My name's Winter. What's your name?"

The little girl replied, "Lilly Rose Lassiter."

Chapter Twenty

Lilly Rose Lassiter . . . Lassiter? Where did this child come from?

She looked strangely familiar, with the red hair that ran through the Lassiter family. Before she could ask Susan about this, a voice behind her spoke to Lilly Rose.

"Lilly Rose, did you knock before coming into Auntie Sue's office, as I asked you to?"

Winter immediately recognized the voice as that of her grandmother. She stood and turned toward the door, and after a long moment of standing and staring at each other, they moved together, lips trembling, tears gathering in their eyes. They hugged, then backed away to look at each other, then hugged again.

Susan came around from her desk to where Lila and Winter stood hugging.

"Both of you better sit down before you fall down. Lila, take some deep breaths. You, too, Winter."

Lilly Rose spoke next. "Grandmother, why are you crying?"

"Oh, Lilly Rose, Winter is someone I love very, very much and have not seen in a very long time. I'm crying happy tears for being able to see her again. Now, how about you going to do your homework and let Winter and me have a visit, then we'll talk about it later?"

"Okay. Have a good visit. I'm glad you're so happy."

And with that, Lilly Rose skipped out of the room—skipped, not walked, just because she could.

Winter reached out to take Lila's hand and began staring at her again.

"Grandmother, Susan has explained a little to me how you and she can look so much younger than your years. I'm so glad. You look just like the last time I saw you, as though all these years had not passed. I've told Susan I want to be the next guinea pig. It's amazing."

"Yes, it is, isn't it? We can't wait for the patent to be issued so that Susan's formula can be released to the world."

"Okay, next question. Tell me about Lilly Rose. Who is she? Who are her parents? What is she doing here? Why did she call you 'Grandmother'?"

It was Susan who fielded that question because of the medical technology involved. As she had done for Lila, she started with the matter of different stem cells, then cloning, then the biobag, then how Lilly Rose was the clone of Winter. No wonder she looked familiar to Winter; she was looking at herself at four years old. Susan explained that she did this four years ago because she couldn't stand to see Lila in such deep depression over the separation from her, and she thought that perhaps a clone of her granddaughter would help her feelings.

"I think I understand," Winter replied. "It's awfully hard to get my head around the fact that when I'm looking at Lilly Rose, I'm looking at myself! And I don't understand why all the secrecy about your death, Grandmother, and why it has been so many years before you let me know you were alive."

Lila explained to Winter, with frequent interjections from Susan. She told Winter about her massive heart attack and that she would not have lived too long after that without a transplant, which, at her age, was not to be possible. Susan chimed in to explain the "heart in a box" and 3D bioprinting, which had just been accomplished once at that point, without time to learn about long-term results.

"But, Grandmother," said Winter, "why wasn't all this explained to me at the time?"

"Winter, within thirty-six hours of my heart attack and transfer here to the laboratory, your father was called and asked to come here. Susan explained everything to him just as she has explained it to you. Legally, it would have required your father's approval for all this surgery to be done. He refused and said that he could not agree to all this risky, unproven stuff that could wind up with my dying anyway. It was for your sake that he felt that since you would have already been told that I had died from a heart attack and you had experienced the trauma of that news, he didn't want to take the chance of additional trauma by telling you I was alive, barely, and then really die, again, when these risky procedures failed. He demanded that all of the equipment I was hooked up to be removed and that I be let to die naturally. Susan didn't do what he requested so that I could be the one to decide whether to proceed with this cutting-edge procedure. As you can see, all went well with the surgery, and there seems to be no ill effects thus far for me or for the others who have gone through the same thing. Understand?"

"Yes, I think so, although I'll have to give the whole thing a great deal more thought. But, why, Grand-mother, let so much time pass before you let me know you were alive?"

"Winter let me get you behind my eyes. All the medical stuff Susan has explained to you took a lot of time. And, since it was only the second time this procedure had been done, there was no way of know-ing if it would work for any length of time. So, in that, I agreed with your father. Better not to let you know that I was alive after you had already dealt with being told of my death than to have you go through it again a second, later time. Then, look back over your life. How could I have interfered with your education, all the way through to your doctorate, with news that would have been so traumatic for you? You had gotten over my so-called death. Why upset you so very badly while you had the pressure of your education? Then, you were in the throes of starting a brand-new practice that required all of your attention. That would not be a good time, either. All of this is not to mention the effect on your father of bringing the news of my being alive. For that reason, I decided to bypass that difficulty by writing the letter to be given to you when both of your parents were deceased. Then what happened? The announcement of your engagement and wedding date was in the paper, which I continued to subscribe to in order to keep up with things in Bliss. Then John and Grace were killed, and you got the letter. Then you and David found each other and quickly married. How could I possibly have you deal with my being alive at that time? But then, David was killed. I read the news of the baby showers given for you, which, of course, told me that you were pregnant. There was no way I would even think about giving you the news during those times. I hope you can see things as I saw them over all these years and understand."

"So, in short, you didn't want to subject me to the possibility of the procedures failing and my being told again that you were dead? Then you didn't want to interrupt any of those times in my life with such a traumatic event? But, Grandmother, I need you to understand how much I needed you to get me through it all."

"We all have twenty-twenty hindsight, Winter. If I was wrong, I'm sorry. You know I would never in a million years have wanted to hurt you, and I was trying to avoid doing that. Now, how has it happened that you have just now called? It's been over a year since John and Grace died."

Winter explained about Ellen having learned about the letter and took it on herself to see that the call was made. There followed talk of Roy and Ellen and showing pictures of Earle. Suddenly, it was almost dark, and Winter had a four-hour drive ahead of her. Before she left, they agreed that there would be frequent visits and that next time she would bring Earle. Many of her thoughts while driving were about Lilly Rose, about her future, about how she would cope with her origin. When she asked about her mommy and daddy, as they all knew one day she would, what was she to be told? This would be the next major topic of discussion with Lila and Susan, only to be followed by one more tragedy and a second major discussion about a life-changing decision.

Chapter Twenty-One

True to her word, the next time she visited Lila, Winter brought four-month-old David Earle Thorpe Jr. with her. It was, of course, thrilling for Lila to see her great grandson, but not as much as it was for Lilly Rose. She begged to hold Earle, looked at him with sheer joy in her eyes, and Winter allowed her to feed Earle his bottle. Earle smiled and cooed at Lilly Rose. An immediate and fierce bond was established between the two of them.

While everyone was having a wonderful visit, it was not to last. Winter got a call from Ellen telling her that Roy had been thrown from a tractor and was badly hurt. Winter, it seemed, was not to escape tragedy in her life. She hurriedly drove to the hospital in Boone, where she found that Roy had died from unstoppable internal bleeding just a few minutes before her arrival. Ellen was inconsolable. Christopher was not much better. Winter asked a nurse to tend Earle while she and Ellen cried and cried together.

Finally, there were no more tears to shed, and they went home to High Hope.

Christopher insisted that his mother spend the night with him and his wife, Caroline, but Winter insisted that she stay the night with her rather than go to her own cottage or with Christopher. Winter won the argument, and after they got Earle settled, the two women sat together with cups of coffee to talk. "My God," Ellen whimpered, "he was sixty-five years old. He shouldn't have even been on that goddamned tractor. I reminded him of why he had hired a younger man to take over those kinds of chores. I tried to talk him out of it, but you know how stubborn he was. He was determined to get that steep hillside mowed. I guess he just forgot about that boulder sticking up. Apparently, one of the tractor tires hit it and caused it to dump over. I don't know why he was so determined to mow that land. It was too steep and rocky for anything to be grown there. He said that's what he had always done and saw no reason to stop doing it."

Between bouts of more tears, they discussed the necessary next steps to be attended to—contacting Roy's family members, funeral arrangements, and so on. Ellen and Roy had years ago purchased plots in the graveyard next to the church they attended. There would, of course, be a reception at High Hope for funeral and burial attendees.

That Lila had not had the opportunity to see Roy again after seventeen years was the source of a great deal of sorrow to her. There was no way she could attend the funeral or the reception. However, the day after the reception, she drove to High Hope. Winter had told Ellen in detail about what she had learned on her previous visits to Zebron, so Ellen was not shocked with Lila's appearance and was happy to see her and grateful that she had come to lend comfort in her grief for having lost her Roy.

Eventually, the discussion turned to what Ellen was to do next with her life. Winter pointed out that just as Roy actually got too old to be doing heavy stuff around the farm, Ellen was the same age and probably shouldn't continue to do all that she did in the house, especially with her taking time to help with Earle. "Winter," Ellen retorted, "what else will I do with myself other than what I have been doing all these years? Taking care of this house is almost as dear to me as taking care of Roy, you, and now Earle." Lila spoke up to say that, regrettably, there was no way she could come back home to help out. She just wasn't up to dealing with everybody who was left in Bliss who thought she had died and had attended her memorial service. No, that just couldn't happen. They ultimately decided to table the subject until they'd all had time to think about it.

Years earlier, Christopher Shands had taken complete control of the pharma-farm High Hope had become, while continuing to supervise building projects from time to time. He made the endeavor very successful, and he had become an expert in pharmacological herbs. Caroline had done a wonderful job with the bookkeeping and other office duties. The office building that was to have been for Winter and David had been completed and was turned over to Chris and Caroline for the pharma-farm business. These were circumstances that were included in Winter's thinking as she mulled over the future for five people—herself, Lila, Lilly Rose, Ellen, and baby Earle.

On one of the next times Winter visited Lila in Zebron, she took Ellen with her. There was something she wanted to let Lila and Ellen know. "You know," she said, "it has fallen on me that as much as High Hope has been my love and the stabilizer of my life, it no longer feels quite the same to me." Lila looked quizzically at Winter and asked, "What do you mean? What do you think has made the difference?"

"High Hope was to have been David's and my home together. I was to have the place and person I loved the most in all the world together, after I thought I had lost my grandmother. After David's death, there is a certain sadness that has become a part of my feelings for High Hope."

"That's understandable," Lila responded. "Winter, I think you are getting at something. What is it?"

"Thinking, Grandmother, just thinking."

"Would you like to tell us what you've been thinking about?"

"Well . . . I look around at the three of us and what I see are three women who have come to a place in their lives when there needs to be a new beginning—perhaps even in a new place."

"A new place? What do you mean a new place?"

Winter turned to Susan, who had joined them. "Susan, could all the medications for your anti-aging protocol be sent to Grandmother wherever she might be?"

"Well, yes, of course, but she would need to be continually monitored, blood tests, et cetera."

"Couldn't that be done with the cooperation of a physician wherever she might be?"

"Yes, I suppose so. But I'd still like to take a look at her myself from time to time. Sounds like you have a plan, Winter. What is it?"

"Okay. Here goes. Please let me finish before the questions start. With Christopher and Caroline's second child, they need more room. Christopher hasn't had time to start building a new home for them. High Hope is five thousand square feet, much too large for me and Earle, and too much for Ellen to continue to take care of. Grandmother, you can't come home again, and it isn't what it used to be for me. I propose—no, too definite—I would have you all think about Grandmother, Ellen, Earle, and I moving someplace else, leaving High Hope to Christopher and Caroline along with the salary Caroline is taking down, and half of the profits from the farm. We can lease Ellen's cottage to vacationers. We could buy a four-bedroom house better suited for all of us. So, what's your initial, knee-jerk reaction?"

Silence.

A long silence.

Finally, Lila spoke. "You've left out Lilly Rose. What's to become of Lilly Rose?"

"Oh, Grandmother, I'm sorry. Of course, Lilly Rose will be with us. We'll get a five-bedroom house to accommodate us all. And I have another idea about Lilly Rose that might solve another problem."

"And what is that?"

"Well, let me go get her, and I'll explain."

With that, Winter left to hunt down Lilly Rose, while Susan and Ellen stared at each other, not knowing what to say. In a few minutes, Winter returned with Lilly Rose, and they sat down. Winter began to talk to Lilly Rose.

"Lilly Rose, we need to talk with you about something."

"Okay, what?"

"Well, you know that you have a grandmother and an aunt, but you don't have a mommy, do you?"

"No. No mommy. Grandmother said when I asked her about it once that we'd talk about it later, but we never did."

"Well, this is that talk. How would it be for you if I were your mommy and Earle was your baby brother? It has been explained to you that your grandmother is actually my grandmother, and she would be your great grandmother. How 'bout that?"

"And you could be my mommy?"

"Yes. And I'd love you just as much as I love Earle."

"And Earle would be my baby brother?"

"Yes, Lilly Rose. That's the way it would be."

"Oh, yes! I would have a mommy and a baby brother. Yes! Yes!"

When Lilly Rose got through jumping up and down and clapping her hands, she hugged Winter, then her "new" great grandmother and her Auntie Sue. Then she asked if Susan would continue to be her Auntie Sue. Winter told her that of course she would, and she would have a new aunt, too, Aunt Ellen. After she was assured about all of that, she turned to leave. Winter asked where she was going. She said she was going to see her baby brother, whom Deborah was taking care of, and off she went, skipping happily.

Winter looked at Lila, who now had tears in her eyes, as well as Susan and Ellen. Finally, Lila said, "Thank you so much for offering to be Lilly Rose's mommy. That just makes me happier than I can tell you. All of what you've said is a lot to think about, Winter. But, I have a question. Have you thought about where we might go?"

Winter replied, "Grandmother, of all our vacations, which was the one we loved the most?"

Lila thought for just an instant, and both she and Winter said at the same time, "*Alaska.*"

Chapter Twenty-Two

From the time Winter was six years old until her last summer vacation when she was fifteen, Lila had taken Winter to myriad places for a vacation: Atlanta, when she was six, for school clothes shopping, followed by trips to Charleston, Orlando, Key West, Maine, California, Canada, Mexico, New Orleans, and, for a few of those years, two trips, to the Bahamas, London, Paris, New York and Niagara Falls, Washington, D.C., and their last trip to Alaska. During all of these trips, Lila took Winter to the finest dining establishments the locations had to offer as well as any museums available. To say that Winter was introduced to the finer things in life is an understatement.

Alaska was a favorite because of the grandeur of its mountains, its history, and its wilderness, along with its urban cities. All this was discussed with Ellen and Susan; meanwhile, Susan investigated the medical and educational facilities in Nome, Fairbanks, Juneau, and Anchorage. It wasn't long before Winter realized that to determine what she actually wanted to know, she would have to make a trip there. But first, there needed to be a conversation with Christopher and Caroline. Winter invited them to dinner at High Hope with her and Ellen. Lila hid with Earle upstairs, with the video part of the monitor turned off.

Christopher and Winter had been close friends since childhood. He had been four years old when Ellen and Roy accepted the jobs at High Hope and moved into the cottage. Winter was just a baby, and he almost thought of her as his baby sister. For many years they shared birthday celebrations, since their birthdays were only two days apart.

Caroline and Christopher met at college. He was studying architecture and construction, and she was studying business administration. Together, they had developed a building contracting business that kept them on a tight budget but that continued to grow. Christopher, having become a pharma-farmer at High Hope, was compensated nicely, which allowed him to continue building as opportunities arose. He assumed that this was to be the topic of conversation at the dinner to which Winter had invited him and Caroline.

Christopher arrived in his "Sunday overalls," as his father had always done for special occasions, including church. Somewhere in the gene pool of his parents, there had to be a gene for height, as Christopher was a tall, sturdy, good-looking young man. Both his parents were relatively short. The three of them had always had a strong, loving relationship, and he always felt part of the Lassiter family.

Caroline was the daughter of a North Carolina farmer, so when she met Christopher, she was quite comfortable with his farming background. He had taken her to High Hope during their courtship. Roy and Ellen liked her immediately and were hoping for their marriage. While Caroline was not a raving beauty, she was very pretty in her fresh-scrubbed face, with no makeup, except a little pale lipstick for special occasions. Coming to dinner at High Hope was a special occasion, for which she chose a sweet dress and let her blonde hair down from its usual pony tail.

They all had pleasant conversation about children, the weather, the crops, and the community rumors, until dessert and coffee. At that point, Winter turned to the real reason she'd invited them for dinner.

"Christopher, Caroline, Ellen and I have asked you to be with us tonight, first because we wanted to spend time with you, but second because there is a change coming that we need to discuss with you, as it involves both of you."

Both Christopher and Caroline put their forks down on their dessert plates and turned their full attention to Winter as she continued.

"You're looking at two widows, and upstairs there is a baby. The circumstances of our lives have changed with the deaths of our husbands, and because of that we need to make some day-to-day living changes."

Looking at his mother, Christopher asked, "What kinds of changes?"

Ellen replied, "Let's let Winter continue explaining."

"Christopher, this is a big house, too big for Earle and me, and too big for your mother to continue taking care of. Your family is expanding. You already have two children, and as you have indicated, both of you loving children, you'd like to have more. The house you are living in is too small for you now, much less with the addition of other children. I know you had been planning to build a larger home when time permitted, but rather than that, Ellen and I would like to see you and your family living here in High Hope."

Christopher and Caroline looked at each other questioningly. Christopher asked, "You mean, with the three of you?"

"No, no," Winter responded. "That would never be comfortable for any of us. What we're suggesting is that we give you this house while we make living arrangements more conducive to our needs elsewhere."

"What kind of 'elsewhere' do you mean? Staying close to us?" Christopher asked.

"Ellen and I need a total change in our lives. This

house no longer means to either of us what it once did for as long as I can remember. We need a complete change of location, a completely new environment for us to live our lives as the widows we are and to raise Earle."

"Well, what kind of location are you thinking of?" Caroline wanted to know.

"As you know, Christopher, Grandmother and I went on vacations every summer. She took me to so many wonderful places, but the one that was my absolute favorite and calls to me even today is Alaska."

"Alaska!" Christopher incredulously exclaimed. "You're proposing taking my mother to Alaska?"

Ellen responded, as she had known this would be how Christopher would take the news. It was she who had to smooth his ruffled feathers. "Whoa. Christopher, Winter is not taking me anywhere. She and I have discussed this at great length, as you might imagine. I remember when Winter and Lila returned from Alaska. We were regaled with their stories and pictures for months. But that isn't the point. Christopher, I'm sixty-five years old. For forty of those years I have taken care of the Lassiter family. Winter is almost as dear to me as you are. I don't want to imagine the rest of my life without her and Earle. It would feel so unnatural, sad and painful. I have lost your father, and to lose Winter and Earle as well would be more than I could bear. You and Caroline have made a life for yourselves. And we would be visiting back and forth several times a year. If being in Alaska is what would make Winter happy, then it will make me happy, and I am just grateful that she wants me to join her. As much as none of us like to think about it, I would be leaving you in the not-too-distant future anyway. This way, you will know that I will be with someone who will love and look after me when I get to the point that I need help. You have always felt as though Winter were your little sister. Likewise, I have always felt that she has been like another child of mine. Winter will continue to need my help, as has been the case for as long as she has lived. Being with her and Earle in Alaska, or anywhere, will give me a kind of normalcy that will be comforting to me."

Christopher and Caroline sat silently, just looking at Winter and Ellen. Finally, Christopher took a sip of his coffee and said, "Mom, I understand everything you have said. The two of you have suddenly dumped this on us, and we are going to need a little time to take it all in and talk about it between us."

"Of course," Winter replied. Ellen nodded in agreement. "I'm sure you have a ton of questions. No decisions need to be made tonight, although Ellen and I have definitely decided to move to Alaska. Why don't we get together again when you feel like it? Just call us when you're ready. Okay?"

Christopher called three days after this shocking meeting. He and Caroline had developed a long list of questions. They came to High Hope, and the four of them sat for a very long time in the living room dealing with all of their questions, mostly about the financial aspects of this change, timing, and the steps to proceed. Winter and Ellen had already anticipated this and were prepared to give answers that would be to their liking. After all the questions were answered, Christopher and Caroline stood, and they all hugged. While Christopher was hugging his mother, he whispered to her that he was not happy about making this sacrifice about being so far away from her, but if this is what she wanted, he would acquiesce. They said good-bye, and Ellen and Winter both wiped a tear or two from their eyes. Lila had gone back to Zebron, and the next step was for Winter to get together with her to begin planning for this monumental move. Except for one other thing that needed to be done: tell David's parents about taking their grandson to Alaska.

Rich and Elizabeth had been very loving and supportive of Winter after David's death. They visited High Hope frequently, and Winter took Earle to see them a couple of times. Winter knew that what she had to tell was going to be tough on them.

Winter called to ask if she and Earle could stop in. They were thrilled, of course, to see their only grandchild. After Earle had been fed, ooh and aahed over, and fallen asleep, Winter broached the subject.

Rich, Elizabeth, there is another reason why I wanted to come visit other than wanting to see you and let you see your grandson. I have news. Can you both come sit on the sofa?" She began explaining all her feelings about High Hope since David's death, and the same for Ellen after Roy's death, ending with the announcement that they had decided to move. Of course, this elicited a question from Rich and Elizabeth: "Move to where?"

When Winter answered Alaska, they first stared at her for a couple of long moments, then looked at each other with questioning faces. "Why Alaska, Winter?" She explained all about when she and her grandmother had visited Alaska, and how it was the only other place in the world they would even have considered living other than High Hope. She was quick to tell them that she would be treating them to spring and fall visits and that she would come to them during the summer, in addition to weekly FaceTiming with them.

Elizabeth began to cry. Rich put his arm around her to comfort her. Winter went to the other side of her on the sofa to assure her that mostly the only difference would be long airplane flights rather than five hours of driving. Rich finally spoke. "Winter, we understand your position and feelings. We only wish there had been some other place, closer, about which you felt as strongly as you do Alaska. That is so very far away. I'm sure I can speak for Elizabeth when I say that we very much appreciate your wanting to accommodate our being able to watch our grandson grow up."

It was at that point that Elizabeth reached to pat Winter's hand, which had been resting on Elizabeth's knee. Although Elizabeth had calmed down and stopped crying, she still wasn't quite able to talk about it. But that pat on her hand told Winter all she needed to know about how they would ultimately feel about the move, as long as they would be able to see their grandchild often. How she would explain Lilly Rose to them when they first visited in Alaska she didn't have a clue. She told herself that she would cross that bridge when she came to it. As her grandmother had told her about worrying about something that had not as yet happened, "Let's don't borrow trouble from tomorrow. We've got plenty enough trouble to be concerned about today."

The next day, Winter and Earle headed to Zebron.

Chapter Twenty-Three

After considerable research, Winter decided on
Eagle River, a small town near Fairbanks. She had
several things to consider in making her choice. First,
it had to be within a reasonable distance to a major city
and airport. Second, it had to provide a medical facility for Lila and a private school for Lilly Rose. Third,
the topography was such that between two mountain
ranges, in the lowlands, the wind could be funneled
between those mountain ranges to very uncomfortable
miles per hour, and the elevation needed to be so that
they would have a beautiful mountain view like they
were accustomed to having at home. Eagle River had
high places and was fairly well protected from the wind.

Winter contacted a real estate agent in Fairbanks
and asked him to find candidates for housing that
would fulfill their needs and desires. But before her trip
to Fairbanks, there was one other thing she needed to
address. She wanted to discuss with Lila taking Lilly
Rose with her. Lila thought it was a wonderful idea

primarily because it would provide an opportunity for Winter and Lilly Rose to bond and establish their relationship as mother and daughter. Lilly Rose was nearly five years old. Her life thus far had been pretty much secluded at Susan's research facility with her and Lila. It was time Lilly Rose was introduced to the rest of the world.

That decision having been made, Winter went to Zebron to talk with Lilly Rose about it. She found her in Lila's cabin reading a book about a little girl who wanted to be a doctor. She was already reading at a sixth-grade level. When Lilly Rose saw Winter walk into the room, her eyes lit up, and she ran to Winter, throwing her arms around her legs. "Mommy!" she exclaimed. And then she asked, "You still are my mommy, aren't you?"

"Well, of course, Lilly Rose. I'll always be your mommy," she replied. "And I have a surprise for you."

"A surprise? Oh, tell me, tell me."

"Lilly Rose, Grandma Lila and your new Aunt Ellen and I have decided that we are all, including you and Earle, going to move. Away from Zebron and away from my home, High Hope, in Bliss."

"Move? Where to?"

"Lilly Rose, we're going to be moving far away."

"Will Auntie Sue be going with us?"

"No, she can't. She has to stay here and continue

doing her research, but she'll be coming to see us a lot. Come here. Let's look at the globe and I'll show you where we will be living."

At the globe, Winter showed Lilly Rose where Zebron was and where Alaska was. She didn't have much of a sense of distances yet, but it still looked like a long way away to her, clear across all the other states. She thought about all of this for a couple of minutes, her little mind racing with questions, then she said, "But we don't have a house there."

"Lilly, that's part of the surprise. I have to go there and find a house for us, and I'd like for you to go with me, if you want to. I think you would enjoy it. We'll be flying in a great big plane, way up high, like the ones we see flying up in the sky, and we'll look down through the windows at the ground and houses and cars and people below. We'll be looking down at our mountains instead of looking up at them. What do you think?"

Lilly Rose had listened intently with her little face screwed up into a frown, trying to take it all in. Winter thought to give Lilly Rose a little time to absorb what she had been told and distracted her with Lila's home-made cookies in the kitchen. They sat together munching on cookies and drinking milk. Lilly Rose had a far-away look in her eyes, deep in thought. Finally, Winter spoke. "So how does all that sound to you? Just you and Mommy taking a trip together?"

"I guess that sounds okay. I'd like for just you and me to be together. When will we go?"

"Oh, in a couple of days. Mommy has to make arrangements for tickets to ride in the airplane, and we need to pack and get ready."

With that settled, Lilly Rose went back to her book, and Winter went back to High Hope. Three days later, Winter picked up Lilly Rose in Zebron and drove to the airport in Raleigh. Winter had bought her a new outfit and a new stuffed animal to establish that this was a very special occasion. Lilly Rose seemed excited, but a little apprehensive, so Winter told her about her visit to Alaska when she was a child and all the beautiful things she had seen and all she had learned. She told her about her favorite place, the Mystic Fjords, which were so beautiful in the mist and perfectly silent. Lilly Rose was listening but distracted by what she was seeing on the way. This was as far away from Zebron as she had ever been. The closer they got to Raleigh, the wider her eyes became. Winter parked the car in long-term parking and collected their luggage, Lilly Rose with her new pull-along, and started off to the airport terminal.

Once inside, panic set in to Lilly Rose. She was completely overwhelmed by all the people, the hustle and bustle and the size of the big building. She grabbed the sleeve of Winter's jacket, pulled hard on it, and began to cry. Winter stopped, knelt down to her, and tried to comfort her. Winter saw seats nearby, so she took Lilly Rose to sit down and talk about it.

"Lilly, here's a tissue. Blow your nose and tell me what's the matter."

"Mommy, I'm scared."

"What are you afraid of, Lilly?"

"All these people. I thought it was going to be just you and me."

"Yes, there sure are a lot of people. Let's look at them. Look at them all coming and going. Some of them just got off of a plane and are trying to go home. Some of them, like us, are going to find our plane and get on it so that we can take our trip. Coming and going. Going and coming." Lilly Rose had stopped crying and was listening to Winter. "Lilly, do you think anything bad is going to happen to you?"

"I don't know. I'm just scared."

"It's okay to be scared, Lilly. Sometimes when you're having a new experience that you don't know anything about, just not knowing can make a person scared. But, after you know about it, the next time you won't be scared. Understand?"

"Okay, Mommy."

"Lilly, you haven't had a mommy before. What do you think mommies do for their children?"

"Love them?"

"That's right. That surely is right. But there's more. We protect our children from anything bad happening to them. While you are having new experiences with me, you must always stay close to me and I'll take good care of you. Okay?

"Okay, Mommy."

"Okay, shall we go find our plane and get in it so we can fly high up into the sky?"

"And look down at the mountains?"

"Yes, look down at the mountains. Let's go now so that the plane doesn't go up into the sky without us."

So off they went. Winter didn't have a free hand to hold Lilly Rose's hand, so she just held on tight to Winter's jacket. Winter continued talking to her along the way, pointing things out to her, explaining what was about to take place. When they had actually gotten on the plane and into their seats, Lilly Rose in a window seat, Winter explained that there was going to be a loud noise as the engines started and they started to move and a loud thunking sound when the wheels went up into the plane. It helped that a stewardess had given Lilly Rose a toy airplane. She had seen how nervous Lilly Rose was. By the time they were airborne and Winter was pointing out things to see through the window, then going up into the clouds, Lilly Rose had become relaxed and excited. It was all going to be okay.

They arrived at the airport in Fairbanks and were met by the real estate agent Winter had contacted. His name was Joel Blanchard; he was tall and very handsome, with a quick and bright smile, blue eyes, and a shock of black hair. After all the introductions, and collecting luggage, Joel took them to his car and on to the hotel where Winter had made reservations, the nicest hotel in Fairbanks. They agreed that he would pick them up the next morning to begin the search for their new home. He had several showings lined up.

It was when Lilly Rose and Winter got into their room that Lilly Rose really became comfortable with her adventure. They decided to have room service for dinner rather than going downstairs to the dining room. Lilly Rose thought this was just great. "Now it really is just you and me, isn't it, Mommy?"

All unpacked, bathed, in their jammies, and snuggled into a big king-sized bed, Lilly Rose drifted off to sleep in Winter's arms, leaving Winter with her thoughts about the day past and the one to come. She smiled when she thought about Joel and how Lilly Rose had warmed to him immediately. She'd asked if he had kids of his own. He'd replied that he had two boys, one about Lilly Rose's age and another two years older. "Your poor wife," Winter commented, "being outnumbered with three males of the species." Joel's face immediately went from smiling to sad. "Cancer took my wife from me six months ago," he said. Winter didn't realize it at the time, but this exchange was her way of determining whether he was married, divorced, or a widower. While she was offering her condolences, deep down inside, hardly noticeable by her, she felt a little twinge of happiness to learn that he was single.

Chapter Twenty-Four

Joel and Winter had agreed to meet for breakfast in the dining room of the hotel the next morning to preview the candidates he had chosen to show them that day. After explaining the primary features of each of four selections, he spread their pictures out on the table. Lilly Rose interrupted eating her pancakes to point at one of them to say, "I like that one."

"Why do you like that one, Lilly Rose?" Winter asked.

"Because it has a big Christmas tree in front of it."

And so it did, a very large fir tree just to the right of the front door. Winter and Joel smiled at each other in appreciation of the mind of an almost five-year-old.

Off they went house hunting. Winter found something unacceptable in the first three that eliminated them from consideration. It was time for lunch, after which Joel would take Winter and Lilly Rose to the Christmas tree house.

Joel took them to one of his favorite restaurants,

a charming seafood café with a beautiful view of the ocean. They had pleasant conversations about what Winter remembered from her childhood visit, what had changed in Fairbanks since then, and whether Winter had seriously considered the dramatic change of weather from North Carolina. "Yes," she assured him. "Winter has always been a favorite season for me. I don't know whether it is because of the name my grandmother gave me, or her reasons for that name, but it has always just appealed to me."

"What were her reasons?" Joel wanted to know.

"Grandmother said that winter was her favorite time of year because everything slowed down then, a break from the busyness of the other seasons, a time to be quiet and take the opportunity to think, plan, remember, and dream. She said that one of her most precious dreams was to have a grandchild. Whether I was to be a boy or a girl, she was determined that the name would be Winter."

"And your parents agreed with that?"

"You have no idea how persuasive my grandmother could be."

"Well, I think it is a beautiful name, different and beautiful."

Winter returned the compliment with a long look into his eyes and a soft "thank you." She thought of adding that she was glad he thought so, but then questioned why she would feel glad. That deep-down feeling she'd had when she'd learned Joel was single returned and rose a little higher in her consciousness.

It was then that Winter chose to ask him about the blue eyes into which she had been gazing. "I just have to ask you. Where did you get your blue eyes? They don't fit with your complexion and hair color."

Chuckling, Joel responded, "I'm half Native. My grandfather was Norwegian, and he immigrated to Petersburg on the coast. Fishing is the prominent industry in Norway, particularly for cod. Norwegian immigrants to Alaska were naturally attracted to good fishing areas like Petersburg. My native ancestors are of the Tlingit tribe, who lived in the Petersburg area and along the coast. The Norwegians and Tlingit women married, producing blue-eyed natives like me. My father was therefore a Norwegian–Tlingit combination. And even though my mother was Norwegian, the Tlingit genes seem to have prevailed in my DNA, except for my blue eyes. It's not really all that rare. You'll see lots of the same in Alaska, mostly in coastal areas."

"How interesting," Winter replied. "Do your boys have blue eyes or brown eyes?"

"You'll probably find this interesting, too. My seven-year-old, Mark, has blondish hair and brown eyes, while the four-year-old has a pale complexion with my black hair and blue eyes."

Lilly Rose interjected with a question of her own. "Mommy, where did my red hair and brown eyes come from?" The question took Winter aback for a moment, but then, regaining her composure, she simply said, "Wherever your red hair and brown eyes came from, it's very lucky for you, because you are so beautiful." Lilly Rose seemed to be satisfied with that answer, smiled, and returned to eating her dessert.

Winter insisted on paying for lunch, but Joel insisted even more strongly and won the argument. Off they went to preview the Christmas tree house.

It was a large house, with a guest cottage attached to the main house by a breezeway, screened in the summertime and glassed in at winter. Its construction was primarily of stone with lots of glass in front for the beautiful mountain views. The roof was steeply pitched to avoid the accumulated weight of snow. The entrance was quite grand, with large French doors with inserts of beveled glass, immediately reminding Winter of the French doors at High Hope that had glass inserts sandblasted with images of tree limbs and leaves. To the left of the entry doors was a stone patio with a stone railing and furnished with comfortable seating and plantings. Very inviting.

Stepping inside, the two-story foyer included an elevator with stained glass in the upper half of the door. To her right was a large living room, full of light from all the windows, beyond which was a dining room in which a table for twelve could be comfortably placed. To her left was a well-appointed bar about half the size of the living room, with coffered ceiling and yet more windows. Beyond the bar was a beautiful office, the walls of which were lined with cherry bookcases. The office had French doors that opened onto another patio. The kitchen was huge with the latest of appliances and appointments and a breakfast nook.

Lilly Rose took it all in quite quickly and was already up the stairs to the balcony that overlooked the foyer and living room. She dashed into each of the bedrooms, and when Winter and Joel arrived upstairs, Lilly Rose took Winter by the hand and pulled her in the direction of one of the bedrooms. "This is my room," she proclaimed. "Oh, really?" said Winter. "And why should this be your room?"

"Because," she explained, "it has a door that goes into the next room, which should be Earle's room so that I can watch over him and play with him."

"Uh huh. I see," said Winter.

The tour continued, revealing that the master bedroom was in the front with mountain views from the windows. Each of the bedrooms had its own private bathroom, with the master bathroom having both a large shower and a Jacuzzi tub. It was delicious!

They moved on to the guest cottage, which was equipped with a small kitchenette, a large bathroom, and a bedroom area open to the living room, with a half wall separating the two areas. It was perfect for Winter's grandmother. The intercom system in the main house included a unit in the guest cottage, so that there could be convenient communication between the two structures.

After taking a look at the two-car garage at the back of the house and the grounds, which included a small garden area and butted up against nothing except forest, Winter looked at Joel and said, "I'd hate to think what I'd give to have it."

Joel smiled and replied, "I'm so glad you like it. I thought it might be just what you were looking for, and besides, it has a Christmas tree in the front yard."

They both nodded and chuckled. Then Joel explained that the house was being sold to settle an estate. The family who had inherited it was very motivated to sell and had just lowered the price. Very fortunately, with the estates of her parents and that of her grandmother, the latter of which had been left intact even though Lila was not dead, and Joel's negotiations, the property was affordable. She had already sent many pictures to Lila and Ellen. They, of course, approved and were excited when Winter advised them that the house had been purchased and was to be their new home. Lilly Rose was ecstatic and began telling Winter about everything she wanted in her room, her room next to Earle's.

Joel and Winter agreed to have a celebration dinner in the hotel dining room just by themselves. Winter left Lilly Rose in their room with Winter's cell phone, but not before showing Lilly Rose how to use it. Winter left her, satisfied to watch a Disney movie, and Winter called to check in with her every little while.

Joel and Winter enjoyed a delightful candlelight dinner, sharing information about their lives. Joel's wife had died of breast cancer six months before. Winter explained David's death and told him all about Earle, High Hope, her grandmother, and the decision to move. She left out all the stories about Lila's supposed death and how Lilly Rose came to be. About Lilly Rose, she simply said that she was born to a Lassiter family member who couldn't care for her, so Winter informally adopted her. They talked about raising children without a spouse, where his boys went to school, and all such things. Finally, it was time for their evening to end, and Joel escorted Winter back to her room. When they got to the door, Winter told Joel, "This has been such a lovely evening." With that, Joel took Winter's hand and held it to his lips for what seemed like a very long time. They said good night.

Winter and Lilly Rose were to leave Alaska the next morning, and Joel insisted he pick them up and take them to the airport. Their good-bye included Winter thanking Joel profusely for helping her find their new home. Lilly Rose, no longer afraid to be in an airport, announced that they would be back soon so that she could move into her new room. Joel picked her up, kissed her on the cheek, and told her how happy he was to have met her and couldn't wait to get her and his sons together for a visit. He put Lilly Rose down, looked longingly at Winter, and gave her a kiss on the cheek as well. "Come back soon," he said. "I will," Winter replied. It was then that she allowed that deep-down feeling to rise completely to the top of her consciousness, and she knew that she was falling in love.

Chapter Twenty-Five

When Winter Lassiter was fifteen years old, she was told that her grandmother, Lila Lassiter, whom she adored, was dead. She was, of course, devastated, and it took a long time for the acute grieving to stop, but there was always a sadness lurking in her heart and mind. Despite this, she managed to graduate from high school, attend and graduate from college, and go on to get her master's and doctorate in psychology. She hung out her shingle as a psychologist specializing in grief therapy. Social life was sporadic and casual.

Then, when she was thirty-two, she met David Thorpe and fell hopelessly in love, followed by eighteen months of mostly heartache and tragedy. First her parents were killed in an automobile accident on their way to High Hope and the wedding. While attending to legal matters pertaining to their deaths, Winter was given a letter from her grandmother, telling her that she was still alive! David and Winter married, and she quickly became pregnant

David and Winter had been married for only six months when he was killed, along with his law partner, by a deranged client who also killed himself. *Why?* Winter just kept asking. *Why?* Why couldn't she be allowed to be completely happy for the first time since she was fifteen? Of course, there was no answer, so she dedicated herself to taking care of her pregnancy and developing a love for David's son growing in her belly. Five months after David's death, baby Earle was born. She had ambivalent feelings about the beautiful baby boy she held in her arms. She loved him desperately, but every time she looked at him, sorrow gripped her for David not being there with them.

Time passed relatively quietly, just enjoying Earle and watching him grow. Given Winter's state of mind at this time, Ellen, the housekeeper and friend who had been a constant in Winter's life, decided on her own that it was time for Winter to deal with the mysterious letter from her grandmother, which included instructions to call a provided phone number. Ellen had been right, and the call was made.

What followed was a visit to Zebron, where Susan, Lila's best and lifelong friend, did medical research in the Lassiter Medical Research Center. As a result of the use of an anti-aging medicinal protocol Susan had created, both Susan's and Lila's aging processes had been halted, and they both looked like they did the last time Winter had seen them. As if this were not enough for Winter to comprehend, during that visit, she was also shocked to meet the four-year-old clone of herself, Lilly Rose Lassiter. It was all just too much to take in. While it had all been explained to her as simply as possible, she had a hard time getting her mind around it. But, at least, shocking though it all was, it was not another tragedy, which, however, was to strike Winter's young life again. Roy, Ellen's husband and the only other constant in her life, was killed in a tractor accident.

For eighteen years, Winter's life had been plagued with tragic deaths, first her grandmother, then her parents, then the husband she adored, then Ellen's husband, Roy. At that point, the only bright spot in her life, other than having Earle, was the knowledge that her grandmother was still alive, though there was considerable angst surrounding that. Having had training in grief counseling was the only thing that allowed her to get through it all. She was her own patient frequently.

Then there came a time when Winter needed a total change. High Hope no longer held the appeal it always had for Winter and Ellen, and the decision was made to leave it to Ellen's son and his family to go . . . where?

Winter had several photo albums stuffed with pictures of her and Lila's trips together, and Winter enjoyed going through them and reminiscing. When she came to their last trip together, to Alaska, there was a special tug at her heart. Finally, it was concluded after much discussion with all involved that Winter, Ellen, Lila, Lilly Rose, whom Winter had adopted as her own, and Earle would move to Alaska. She had no way of knowing that this was the most fortuitous decision she had ever made and was grateful that the other widows agreed to join her. It was most fortuitous because it was in connection with finding suitable housing in Alaska that love came into her life again, in the person of Joel Blanchard, the realtor who had helped her find the house and whom Lilly Rose instantly liked. And to whom she found herself surprisingly attracted.

After locating and purchasing their new home in Alaska, there was much to do about furnishing it. Winter decided to make another trip for that purpose, only this time she would go alone, leaving Lilly Rose, much to her chagrin, back in Zebron with Lila and Susan.

When she arrived in Fairbanks, Joel met her at the airport. Their greeting included a long hug and looking into each other's excited eyes. He took her to the same hotel where she had stayed before. Before going upstairs, they stopped at the bar to have a drink and a chat. They talked about things pertaining to the house, how his kids and Lilly Rose were all doing.

Then he reached his hand across the table to hers and told her that he couldn't believe how much he had missed her since they had been together previously, and how thrilled he was when he heard that she was to return. Winter realized that he was saying what had been true for her as well, and she told him so with a simple, "Me, too."

There followed a flurry of activity going to furniture stores, visiting paint stores, hiring a painter, sifting through wallpaper stores, and hiring a wall paper hanger, all with constant contact via cell phone with her interior designer grandmother. Winter had asked Joel about the location of a car rental place, but he insisted that he was to be her chauffeur while she attended to her furnishing business. "But what," she asked, "are you to do while I am spending hours picking out furniture. You do have a business to run, don't you?" He told her that he would drop her off to the places she needed to go, and if she was to be there for long, she was to call him when she was done, and he would pick her up. He further told her that he wanted to spend as much time with her as he could. This included breakfast, lunch, and dinner, sometimes at the hotel, sometimes at Joel's favorite places. Each day he would escort her back to her room, kiss her on the cheek, and say good night, until the third day she was there. On that evening, she returned his kiss on the cheek with a kiss on the lips she had been longing to feel against hers. Except for the fact that he had left his boys with a baby sitter, she would have invited him into her room that very night. It wasn't long thereafter, however, that arrangements were made for him to spend the night with her. What they both thought might be awkward, this being the first foray into sex for both of them since the deaths of their spouses, was not. It seemed as comfortable and natural as though they had been together for a long time.

After spending a week buying all the furniture the house would need for the five of them, arranging to have utilities turned on, and all those things moving into a new home entailed, it was time for her to go back to North Carolina. Their good-bye at the airport was poignant and lasted until the last moment for her to take her seat on the plane. She promised that she would be back as soon as possible, and this time with all the widows she had told him about, as well as Lilly Rose, with whom she had spoken every night while they were apart. What she had not told him about were the most unusual circumstances about her grandmother and Lilly Rose. She was anxious about what effect this would have on their new relationship. She felt she needed a little more time before she dropped that bomb on him.

When she got to Zebron, Lilly Rose greeted her with tight hugs and lots of kisses. Everyone was excited about the Alaskan adventure they were about to begin. After all the welcoming was over, Winter was anxious to have a few moments with Lila, to tell her about Joel. Lila was pleased and happy that Winter had found love again. Her comment was, "Winter, by this time you have lived through enough tragedy and trauma to realize that love is the only thing this ridiculous thing we call a lifetime is worth trying to keep, as I continue to do for love of you and Earle and Ellen and Susan and Lilly Rose." Winter was excited to tell Joel on the phone for their nightly call how her grandmother had received the news about him.

Chapter Twenty-Six

Meanwhile, winter was not too long in coming in Alaska, which meant more shopping for her and Lilly Rose for a wardrobe appropriate for Alaskan winters. Winter spent a lot of time shopping online for more furnishings for the new house, having them all sent to Joel's office for him to take to the house. She began to feel pressured from both Joel and Lilly Rose to make their final trip to their new home. Lila and Ellen were agreed that they should go ahead of them. Anything left to be done could be done from Alaska. Susan agreed to go this time as well, so that she could make arrangements for Lila's care and monitoring with a physician she had already contacted, whom she felt sure was going to take care of Lila and would periodically receive the "special medication" to administer to her.

Winter and Ellen, having had dinner with Christopher and Caroline during which they talked about the house, let them know that it was okay to dispose of and replace any of the furniture in the house. Winter had only one thing shipped to Joel's office—her grandmother's portrait. So, after a tearful good-bye and the promise that they would come to Alaska for a visit in spring, Christopher and Caroline left. Ellen and Winter sat together quietly for a while, both of them lost in their thoughts and memories of life at High Hope. Then, remembering that they were going to have a long day the next day flying to Fairbanks, they needed to get some sleep. There wasn't much sleep to be had, however. It was all too dismaying and exciting to allow for sleep. The day after their arrival in Fairbanks was Friday, when Winter and Joel could have the weekend together, and to make introductions between him and Winter's family, and Winter with Joel's family, all of which was very well received.

After getting settled in the Christmas tree house, the next thing on the beginning-a-new-life agenda was for Winter to establish a relationship with Joel's boys. A new indoor recreational facility in Fairbanks had just opened for business, so Winter and Joel took the boys there to have some fun with them and get to know each other a little. That having gone well, many more times together, along with Lilly Rose, were enjoyed until everyone was comfortable with everyone else.

One day, while the children were playing, Joel said,

"There's something I have been meaning to talk to you about, concerning Eller."

"Eller?"

"Oh, yeah, I forgot to tell you about that. Timmy was having a hard time pronouncing Lilly Rose's name, with all the *L*s following each other in 'Lilly.' When they told me about that problem, I suggested that they just call her 'Rose.' When they suggested this to Lilly Rose, she nixed that idea. Next I pointed out that many people were called by the initials of their names—in Lilly Rose's case, it would be 'L.R.' Surprisingly, Lilly Rose agreed to that, but 'L.R.' soon morphed into 'Eller,' and that's what they have been calling her; I guess I picked it up, too."

"Hmm. I see. And is Lilly Rose okay with that?"

"She seems to be. She answers to it as though she had always been called that."

Winter chuckled, then said, "Okay. I'll fly it by Grandmother, names being so important to her. But you started out telling me that there was something you wanted to discuss with me about . . . Eller."

"Yes. I've been thinking about that little girl having been through so much in the last several months. So many challenges and changes. That's always the source of some degree of stress. I'm thrilled that she and the boys have quickly become so close. They talk about Eller all the time."

"Yeah, I'm so pleased about that, too. Being an only child has its drawbacks."

"So what I've been thinking about is a special surprise for Eller."

"Oh, yeah? Like what?"

"I want to get her a puppy. In fact, I'd like to get two puppies, a male and a female, for all of them to enjoy."

"They will live at my house?"

"Yes, Winter, of course, with the hope that it will be our house one day for all of us."

One day. She just smiled and determined that "one day" would not be too far off. "Oh, Joel, I think that would be wonderful of you. She will be thrilled. All of them will. There's only one thing I'd like to ask you."

"Yeah? What's that?"

"Are you going to help pick up puppy poop 'til they're housebroken?"

"Of course," he replied, and they sealed that decision with a kiss.

One night at supper, Winter asked Lilly Rose about her new name.

"So, Lilly Rose. I understand that you have been given a new nickname, 'Eller.' Is that okay with you?"

"Yes, Mommy, that's okay. And you can call me Eller, too."

"Grandmother, what do you think about that?"

"Well, Eller Lassiter. I like it. Very melodic."

And so Eller it was to be. No one could have known at that time that Eller Lassiter Blanchard would be a name history would recall with shock and awe.

Next, Joel and Winter got together with all his family—his parents, his sister, aunts, uncles, and other members of a large family. Without exception, they all seemed very happy for Joel that he had fallen in love with Winter and made her feel welcome in their family.

Chapter Twenty-Seven

As fall approached, three major things happened. First, true to his word, Joel showed up one day with two puppies. They were cross breeds between a German shepherd and an Alaskan husky. Joel said he was immediately attracted to them because they came from two lineages, just like himself, and because one got the shepherd's brown eyes and the other got the husky's blue eyes, just like his boys. Then, there was the issue of what to name them. Lilly Rose opined that the one with blue eyes should be called "Blue." That made sense and was acceptable to everybody. The boys got their heads together and decided on a name for the brown-eyed puppy. What they came up with was "Shep," because it looked more like a German shepherd. So Blue and Shep it was, and the children were beside themselves with joy.

The next major thing that happened was not joyful—Lila made the announcement that she no longer wanted to extend her lifetime. It had come time for Winter to take Lila to the doctor who was giving her the medicine Susan had prepared. Lila balked at going and said, "Winter, I have come to a decision. I'm going to stop taking Susan's meds. I've discussed it with Susan, and she has agreed with my decision and reasoning."

"But, Grandmother, why? It's working so well for you."

"Winter, I have lived longer than I was supposed to. There is something about the natural order of things, beginning, middle, and end, that is appealing. It is predictable. I understand your father's point of view. I'm seeing you deliriously happy, and that seems to me to be my exit cue. It is what I had hoped for since the day you were born. Besides, I am getting increasingly curious about what my life as a spirit will be. Maybe I'll go haunt someone."

"Oh, Grandmother, you're not going to go haunt anybody. Are you very sure about this?"

"Yes, dear, very sure. Susan was sorry to lose her guinea pig, but she has many, many more now."

"Do you have any idea how much I'm going to miss you? After having lost all those years with you? And now you are to go away again?"

"Winter, you got through the first go-round, and this time, you're going to be too busy with your new family to give much thought to me."

Winter sat for a few moments just looking at Lila, holding her hand, shedding a tear that insisted on being released to run down her cheek. "Grandmother, I think I understand your feelings, and whether I do or not, it is your life. You have made some monumental decisions about your life. I'll accept yet another. Most reluctantly."

Lila reached to cradle Winter's face in her hands. "Winter," she said, "remember what I have taught you about there really being no such thing as death, only a change of states of being. And whatever state I am in, I'll always stay close to you and the family." She gave Winter a kiss on the cheek, then told her to go see what the rest of the family was doing.

What they were doing was various things. The boys were playing some game. Eller was helping Ellen make cookies. And Earle was crawling around on the floor finding, then throwing, his toys, then crawling to find them again. He was trying to walk, so as to get into as much trouble as he could.

When Joel came that evening, Winter told him about the conversation between her and Lila. She was obviously upset, so Joel went to the chair in which she was sitting, grasped her hands, and pulled her up. "Come on, honey. Let's go for a walk. The fall leaves are getting beautiful, and it will be spring before we know it. New beginnings. Another new beginning for us to experience, together."

That was exactly what Winter needed at that particular moment. She had always loved the autumn leaves. She said it made all the dreary winter trees and shrubs look beautiful before spring greened them up. It happened to be a sunshiny fall day. They strode to a little knoll and stood holding each other and gazing out at the mountain view. But it wasn't long before Blue and Shep and all the big kids found them and scampered up the knoll to be with them. "Look at them all," Joel said. "They're all a bunch of mixed up mongrels!" Winter playfully elbowed him and chuckled.

Chapter Twenty-Eight

They made their way back to the kitchen, to the aroma of cookies baking.

This was not the last time the kitchen would send the aroma of baking cookies throughout the house. Winter had hired cleaning ladies to take care of the rest of the house, under Ellen's supervision, but the kitchen was her domain. She maintained that there was nothing so gratifying as feeding the people she loved.

The third major thing to happen that fall, as Winter had hoped, was Joel's solid proposal that they legitimize the blending of their families by getting married. Winter was not surprised with this turn of events. He had already made references to it, and they had discussed the matter and how the house might accommodate three new members to the household. More importantly, she knew this was the time to tell Joel about the unusual aspects of her family.

She explained about Lilly Rose, who was the clone of herself. Joel's eyes were wide open as she recounted how this had all taken place. She explained as best she could about Susan and her anti-aging protocol. She explained more of her own life, being told of the death of her grandmother, and then the letter saying she was not dead. Joel listened intensely and nodded his acknowledgment of what Winter was saying.

Finally, Joel responded. "As I understand it, that means I'm going to have two of you, in my wife and my daughter. Well, won't that be just wonderful." All Winter could do was cry while Joel held her in his arms. She tried to speak to tell him how grateful she was for his response to all of this weird stuff, and how much she loved him, but every time she released herself from his arms and looked into eyes, she just couldn't help but start crying again. She really didn't need to say anything. Joel interpreted her tears correctly—as an expression of relief and love. Their hearts bonded even more closely.

Joel proposed in such a sweet way. The next morning, he asked if he and the boys could stop by on their way to school to see her and Eller, who was still being home-schooled. Of course, she agreed. When they got there, the boys stood together with Joel standing behind them, his hands on their shoulders, and he said, "We have all talked it over and want to know if you two would agree to let's put your family together with our family to become one family. Lilly Rose, would it be okay with you if I asked your mommy to marry me and share her with me and the boys? And would you like it if I became your daddy, and you could call me Daddy, just like the boys?" Lilly Rose jumped up and down and yelled "yes!" not once, but twice.

Taking the cue of how Joel wanted to pursue this proposal, Winter stepped forward and addressed the boys. "Would you like to have Lilly Rose and Earle as your sister and brother and me as your mom? Understand that I cannot and would not replace the mother you lost. That would not be possible. But I could love you as much as she did and as much as I love Lilly Rose and Earle. And if I am to be your mommy, you could call me Mommy just like Eller does. How 'bout that?" Their response was not as exuberant as Lilly Rose's had been, but with one "yep," a lot of smiles, and nodding in the affirmative, Joel went to Winter, got down on his knee in the traditional manner, produced an engagement ring, and said, "Winter. You have stolen the hearts of me and my boys. We want you to be in our lives forever. I love you so much. Would you do us the honor of becoming my wife and their mom?"

So, in response to Joel's marriage proposal, with a twinkle in her teary eyes, she responded, "How long do I have before I answer?"

"Not one second," Joel replied.

"Well, then, I guess I better say yes right away. All

of you have stolen my heart as well, and I would be thrilled to be your wife and," looking at the boys, "your mom."

With that, Joel rose to put the ring on Winter's finger, and they kissed for a long, loving moment, with all the kids gathered around hugging them.

Chapter Twenty-Nine

Winter wanted to plan the date of their wedding with Christopher and Caroline's visit, to take place there at what would be called the "Christmas Tree House" forever. Spring was always a very busy time for them with the farm and Christopher's building projects, but they finally agreed on May 24 to be the wedding day, which arrived preceded by all manner of preparation. Rich and Elizabeth had already planned a spring visit for a little later. Winter brought them up to date with what had happened in her life, that she and Joel were to be married, and that she would love to have them attend and meet their grandson's stepfather. True to their nature, they accepted the idea and changed their plans for travel accordingly.

As to Eller, it was concluded that they would be told the same story that Susan had told her staff at the research center—a member of the Lassiter family had brought Eller to Lila because the mother couldn't care for her, she had no other family, and Winter had adopted her to be her own daughter. And that would be that, for the time being.

Winter and Joel struggled over the decision whether Joel and the boys should move in with Winter, Lila, and Ellen before their marriage. What would the older ladies think of this? What kind of example would they be setting for the children? After discussing it with all parties concerned, and in consideration of the risk of winter roads for traveling back and forth, it was concluded that, since they were already married in their hearts, this would be the reasonable thing to do.

One of the rooms in the main house was used by Ellen. To accommodate Joel's two boys, it was agreed that this would be their room, and Ellen would share the cottage with Lila. It turned out to be right cozy for Ellen and Lila, and besides, it made Winter happy to know that her grandmother was not alone in the cottage.

Meanwhile, Lila's skin got thinner every day, her wrinkles deeper, her auburn hair changing from the few streaks of white at her temples to all white, her hearing and vision deteriorating; she agreed to a walker to help support and steady her. She had desperately wanted to be present for the wedding, but almost four months after she refused to continue Susan's regimen, Ellen found Lila in their cottage, dead in her bed.

Winter decided to have a small immediate family

gathering to memorialize Lila's passing. She was the only speaker, and despite a few moments of quivering lips and a tear to be wiped away, she got through it. Mostly for Joel and the boys, she told Lila stories—about her love of High Hope, about the special love between her and Lila, about their vacations together, which is what brought them to Alaska.

Lila was cremated, and before the wedding, Winter took her ashes to High Hope to be scattered. She did this alone, without Joel, Lilly Rose, Christopher, or Caroline. She didn't want to explain whose ashes those were. One afternoon, she just scattered them in the rose garden. She explained her visit by saying there was a business matter she needed to resolve, and actually there was, which was the explanation to everyone except Joel and Earle, of course, for her abrupt departure.

Lila's friend Celia had turned the antique store they owned together over to her daughter. Now, her daughter, having gone through a divorce, had found love again and was to be married in a month or two. No one else in the family was interested in running the store, so Celia wanted to sell the business and property.

Winter could certainly relate to Celia's daughter's turn of events in her life. Winter quickly agreed to put the business and property on the market and told Celia she would contact a commercial realtor immediately.

She also confirmed that since she and Lila had been equal partners, 50 percent of the proceeds of the sale would go to her. That had been a question in Celia's mind, but she didn't know how to broach the subject with Winter, who, through inheritance, actually owned the business. She was very grateful for Winter having told her the manner in which things were to be handled. It was actually no surprise. She had known Lila so well and was aware of the closeness between Lila and Winter. Lila was the most fair, honest person she had ever known. She felt sure Lila had passed those traits on to Winter.

Scattering Lila's ashes served as a closing of that chapter of her life. Lila had reminded her that the more people you love, the more opportunity there is for heartbreak. During the last twenty-two months, the number of people she loved was increased by Earle, Joel, Tim, and Mark—and Lilly Rose. She prayed—hard—that no further tragedy would befall her. She'd had enough. She could only foresee two more challenges in her life: Ellen's death and explaining to Lilly Rose her origins. She hoped the latter would be much further away, when Lilly Rose was much older and more capable of dealing with what was, no doubt, going to be very traumatic for her. When that time came, Winter would hold Lila to her word that she would stay close to her and help her know the right and best way to meet this challenge. "At least," she thought, "I'll have Joel to help get us both through it." And so she hurried back to him.

Chapter Thirty

Lila had, despite becoming increasingly frail, decorated the house beautifully for the wedding and was thrilled that Susan agreed to come, although as it happened, Susan came after the wedding. Ellen had been working on recipes for canapes for days. Special new outfits were purchased for the wedding party, including little Earle, who was by then almost eighteen months old. Winter chose a long, lacy, mint green dress and had baby's breath woven into an updo of her auburn hair.

The wedding was officiated by one of Joel's best friends, who was a notary public. Lilly Rose was the flower girl; Timmy, Joel's younger son, was the ring bearer, and Mark was Joel's best man. Ellen served as Winter's matron of honor.

Winter walked down the "aisle," which was from the kitchen and through the dining room to the living room, where Joel was waiting for her in front of the fireplace.

After the opening parts of the ceremony, Joel and Winter spoke their vows to each other.

"Winter, I never dreamed that I would find love again, and here you are, with your heart open to me, Mark, and Tim. I promise to love and cherish you for as long as we both shall live."

"Joel, here you are standing before me, your heart opened to me and Eller and Earle, and I promise to love you for as long as we both shall live."

When it came to the pronouncement, Joel and Winter had something special added. Joel's friend looked at the boys and asked, "Mark, Tim, do you take Winter to be your mom and promise to love and honor her as such?" As they had been prompted to do, they both replied, "We do."

"And Lilly Rose, I mean Eller, speaking for yourself and Earle, do you take Joel to be your dad and promise to love and honor him as such?"

"Yes, yes, yes!" Eller excitedly replied.

"With that I now pronounce you husband and wife, father and mother, and family."

Winter and Joel stood looking into each other's eyes for a long moment. Having experienced so much pain in the previous eighteen months, this moment for Winter was as intensely happy as all the others put together were tragic. Their kiss was long and tender. There wasn't a dry eye in the house, except for the children, who, at Lilly Rose's instigation, gathered together and hugged—the most poignant moment of the whole day.

The festivities that followed were especially enjoyable. Rich and Elizabeth warmly accepted Joel and Lilly Rose to be a part of their lives as well, through the mutual love of Earle. They were happy that Earle would have a father help raise him and to love him. They told Lilly Rose that Earle was their grandson and asked her if she would like to be their granddaughter. Of course, Lilly Rose smiled and nodded in agreement. From that day forward, whatever gifts were given to Earle, the same was done for Lilly Rose, as well as Mark and Timmy.

At one point, Winter and Joel stood apart from the crowd and smiled at each other. They were looking at family, the blending of families, chatting going on between members of each of their families, strange as the history of one of them was. Rich and Elizabeth didn't need to know, nor did Joel's family. She was just a little girl who apparently had gotten all of the Lassiter genes, as she looked like she could be Winter's own flesh and blood—which, of course, she was.

THE END